Selected Stories of Xiao Hong

Translated by Howard Goldblatt

Panda Books

Panda Books
First Edition 1982
Second Printing 1987
Copyright by CHINESE LITERATURE PRESS
ISBN 7-5071-0008-1/I·9
ISBN 0-8351-2054-6

Published by CHINESE LITERATURE PRESS, Beijing (37), China
Distributed by China International Book Trading Corporation
(Guoji Shudian), P.O. Box 399, Beijing, China
Printed in the People's Republic of China

This book is dedicated to the members of Harbin's literary community

Acknowledgments

OF the nine stories included in this collection, three have been previously published in anthologies of modern Chinese short stories. "Hands" and "The Family Outsider" were included in Joseph S. M. Lau, C. T. Hsia, and Leo Ou-fan Lee, eds., *Modern Chinese Stories and Novellas, 1919-1949* (New York: Columbia University Press, 1981); "On the Oxcart" appeared in Vivian Ling Hsu, ed., *Born of the Same Roots* (Bloomington: Indiana University Press, 1981). "Spring in a Small Town" is a slightly altered version of the original translation by Sidney Shapiro, which appeared in *Chinese Literature* No. 8, 1961.

Xiao Hong's best known and perhaps most artistic story, "Hands", has been published in two earlier translations, but I have found it advisable to present it here in a totally new translation.

Many people have contributed both to my understanding of the stories included here and to the quality of the translations. To them, particularly Professor Joseph Lau of the University of Wisconsin and Judi Wong of San Francisco State University, I extend my thanks. I also wish to thank Miss Lu Weiluan of the Chinese University of Hong Kong, who not only discovered the story "North China" in a Hong Kong magazine, but who also made it available to me.

Finally, I hope that by dedicating this volume to the many writers, scholars, and teachers of Harbin, who have devoted years of work to giving Xiao Hong the recognition she so richly deserves, I can express a measure of appreciation for the support and encouragement they gave me during my two trips to their lovely city.

HG
Los Angeles

Introduction

IT is generally agreed that the reputation of a novelist is not always well served by anthologies of his (or her) short stories, for the two genres are so radically different that few writers have been able to master both. Xiao Hong seems to be a notable exception, for two compelling reasons: the novels for which she is justifiably famous among modern Chinese writers tend to be so episodic and cinematic that one can often discern the essence of one or more short stories buried in the body of the novels;* and the themes, character types, and writing styles of both her short and long works have marked similarities.

Given what we know of Xiao Hong's life and artistic temperament,** including the fact that while she was physically ill and caught up in the war with Japan, she wrote one full-length novel and the first two volumes of a planned trilogy, we must conclude that she

---

* Her first novel, *The Field of Life and Death* (*Shengsi chang*), was published in 1935. Part I of *Ma Bole* was published in 1940, while Part II appeared the following year in serialized form in a Hong Kong literary magazine. *Tales of Hulan River* (*Hulanhe zhuan*) was published in 1941. All of these novels have recently been republished by the Heilongjiang People's Publishing House. Translations of *The Field of Life and Death* and *Tales of Hulan River* (two volumes in one) have appeared in the Indiana University Press translation series (1979).

** See Howard Goldblatt: *Hsiao Hung* (*Xiao Hong*), Boston, 1976.

was by nature a novelist, a writer who required a broad canvas on which to create her most memorable literary works. However, as any student of modern Chinese literature knows, it was far easier and more expedient to write short stories, which could be sold to the many literary journals of the day — keeping the wolf from the door was always an urgent concern of twentieth-century Chinese writers, particularly during the 1930s and 1940s. So for six of Xiao Hong's nine creative years she wrote nothing but short stories, essays, and an occasional poem or short play. Yet she is known primarily as a writer of novels, the first of which (*The Field of Life and Death*) she wrote at the age of 23, the final two of which (three, if Parts I and II of *Ma Bole* are counted separately) were written shortly before her death nearly a decade later.*

In thematic terms, Xiao Hong generally deals with the plight of women from the deprived classes; her stories are almost invariably tragic and seldom offer much hope for change. As a woman who felt herself demeaned, abused, and valued primarily as a feminine object by the men with whom she was associated, Xiao Hong was revolutionary in her desire to expose the cruelties in a male-dominated "feudalistic" society. Her

---

* Xiao Hong was born in Hulan County, Heilongjiang Province in 1911. After attending high school in Harbin, she ran away from her landlord family, eventually settling down with the Northeastern writer Xiao Jun. They both fled the Japanese occupation of Manchuria in 1933, travelling to Shanghai, where they came under the wing of Lu Xun (1881-1936). Following the outbreak of war with Japan, Xiao Hong went to the interior, where she left Xiao Jun and married another Northeastern writer, Duanmu Hongliang. In 1940 she and Duanmu flew to Hong Kong, where Xiao Hong died two years later, on January 22, 1942. Her remains are now buried in the city of Guangzhou.

stories are extremely touching and evocative, and, we can assume, effective tools in the awakening process that characterized the period during which she lived and wrote. Most of her stories are set in northeast China, although only a few (including the first story in the present anthology, her first work of fiction) were written there. The only notable exceptions are the stories in her volume *A Cry in the Wilderness*, which are set in the Chinese interior. In only three of the nine stories included here do men play the leading role, and one of these — "The Family Outsider" — is a piece of autobiographical fiction.* To take this last point further, a large percentage of Xiao Hong's fictional works, which are told in the first-person narrative mode, are more or less autobiographical, the narrator being a secondary character.

If there is one story that seems out of place here and in Xiao Hong's corpus generally, it is "Flight from Danger"; with a male protagonist, and written in a satirically humorous vein, it is like nothing else Xiao Hong wrote up to that time. It is, however, the story upon which the trilogy she began but never completed — *Ma Bole* — is based.

Taken together with her novels, the short stories included here should strengthen the claim that Xiao Hong was not only a first-rate story-teller and an artist who painted vivid scenery in words, but a literary genius whose potential was never realized owing to a lack of editorial assistance, the difficult times in which she lived, and her tragic death at the age of thirty.

---

* This story is the basis for chapter six of *Tales of Hulan River*

Bibliographic Note

THE stories in this anthology are arranged in chronological order. All but the story, "North China", have appeared in anthologies of works by Xiao Hong, as follows:

"The Death of Wang Asao": *Trudging* (*Bashe*), Harbin, 1933, co-authored by Xiao Jun. Reprinted by the Heilongjiang Branch of the Chinese Writers' Association in 1979.

"The Bridge" and "Hands": *The Bridge* (*Qiao*), Shanghai, 1936.

"On the Oxcart" and "The Family Outsider": *On the Oxcart* (*Niuche shang*), Shanghai, 1937.

"Flight from Danger" and "Vague Expectations": *A Cry in the Wilderness* (*Kuangye de huhan*), Chongqing, 1939.

"Spring in a Small Town": *Spring in a Small Town* (*Xiaocheng sanyue*), Hong Kong, 1961.

"North China" was published in a Hong Kong newspaper in 1941.

CONTENTS

The Death of Wang Asao	13
The Bridge	28
Hands	46
On the Oxcart	69
The Family Outsider	84
Flight from Danger	131
Vague Expectations	143
North China	155
Spring in a Small Town	189

The Death of Wang Asao

THE grass and the leaves of plants were covered with a layer of gray-white frost. The yellow-leaved trees on the mountain were waiting for the morning sun, and when it appeared over the horizon, it gave rise to a rosy dawn. Flowers and grass in the wild pastureland gave off an aroma that was filled with the chill and desolation of autumn.

The wildflowers, tiny stream, and grass huts were obscured by a cloud-like layer of fog which obliterated all sound and even blotted out the surrounding hills, far and near.

Just before sunrise each morning Wang Asao went out with Little Huan to the square of the front village to slave away for the landlord. Little Huan may have only been seven years old, but she was already learning how to serve the landlord as a slave-child. Spring had come and gone, summer had come and gone... Wang Asao had performed every type of work imaginable, including weeding the fields and planting rice shoots. Now that autumn had arrived she sat with the other village women under the overhanging rush roofs using lengths of hemp cord to make string after long string of eggplants. None of them paid any attention to the mosquitoes and other insects that continued to bite their already swollen faces and hands any more than they did to the children screaming for their mommies from inside the huts. They were preoccupied with threading the fruit, their hands weaving back and forth like looms, making one string after another.

On the following morning the strings looked more like threads of purple beads than eggplants as they hung from the eaves in front of Wang Asao's hut, from one end to the other. Even the low willow-branch fence that encircled her hut was literally covered with strings of purple beads. It was the same with all of her fellow village women: row upon row of strung-up eggplants hung from the eaves of their huts.

After hanging in the sun for several days, the eggplants had dried, and all the families in the neighborhood started taking them down and delivering them to the landlord's storeroom. When winter came, all that Wang Asao would have to eat were rotten potatoes that the landlord used as pigfeed. Not a single slice of dried fruit ever found its way into her mouth.

The eastern sun slanted directly into the workers' eyes. As the fog burned off, gradually exposing the surrounding hills, the men and women in the fields increased their work pace. Clusters of goats and oxen foraged among the wild grasses that were beginning to wither in the autumn frost in the pastureland and on the hillsides.

Wang Asao was nowhere to be found in the field. That was puzzling. Third Master Zhu came out to the square every morning to pass out the work assignments for Landlord Zhang. On this occasion, he told a young woman who was picking potatoes to go look for Wang Asao.

The work-team leader, Lengsan, broke in with:

"You'd better send me instead. A man can get it done faster."

Two minutes after Third Master Zhu had given his approval, Lengsan was standing outside Wang Asao's window.

"Wang Asao, why aren't you out working?"

There was an immediate response from inside the hut:

"I'm sure glad you're here, Uncle. Would you run over and ask Sister Wang to come over here from the front village. I have such a splitting headache I won't be able to work today."

Little Huan, who was sitting at Wang Asao's side, blurted out through her tears:

"Mommy's lying. She can't go to work 'cause her belly's so big. She cried all night long, but I don't know if it's 'cause her belly hurts or 'cause she was thinkin' 'bout Daddy."

Little Huan's words pierced her mother's heart, pierced it to its very core. She swallowed her tears as she patted Little Huan's head impatiently to get the child to stop talking.

Li Lengsan was a cousin of Wang Asao's husband. Little Huan's outburst seemed to have touched off some familiar sympathies in him, for he dashed off to the front village without hesitation.

Little Huan climbed up onto the window ledge and fussed with her tiny, mussed-up braid with hands that still didn't know how to comb her own hair. A kitten from next door jumped up onto the ledge, where it curled up in the little girl's lap. Seemingly trying to find some warmth, the kitten lay there lazily opening and closing its eyes.

A rainbow of early morning colors was reflected off the distant hills. The cluster of grazing goats and oxen appeared as tiny black specks moving about in the rosy clouds. But Little Huan was too busy fussing with her mussed-up braid to notice any of this.

2

In the villages people referred to one another with names like Sister Wang, Lengsan, and Third Master Zhu. Working-class people customarily use such simplified forms of address, forms that never change. This is a natural symbol of the working class.

Sister Wang sat at Wang Asao's side, while Little Huan squatted on the *kang*; a sense of loneliness gripped all three of them. When the sun was directly overhead, a horde of insects — whatever they were — set up an unbearable din on the hill behind the hut, the sound a mixture of comic laughter and resentful sadness.

Although she was only seven, Little Huan already knew what it was like to experience sadness and to be pensive, just like a young lady. As she listened to the chirping insects, she imitated the two adults by pouting with her tiny mouth and sighing. Perhaps all of this was a direct result of her having lost her mother at such a tender age.

Little Huan's father had been a hired hand who had died before she was even born. Then when she was a child of five she had lost her mother, who had died of humiliation after being raped by Zhang Huqi, Landlord Zhang's son.

So Little Huan had become a homeless waif at the age

of five. She had lived for a while with some impoverished paternal relatives, then had been bundled off to some maternal relatives who were, if anything, even worse off. Their poverty had made it impossible for them to take care of her, so she had spent a year of torment in the home of Landlord Zhang. Third Master Zhu had agonized over the sight of Little Huan suffering such abuse. Then one day Wang Asao had come over to the Zhang home to fetch some rice just after Little Huan had received a bloody nose from Landlord Zhang's children; she was just standing there, her face covered with blood. Wang Asao had thrown down her sack of rice in the courtyard, walked over to the little girl, and wiped the blood and tears from her face. Little Huan was crying; so was Wang Asao.

From that day onward, Wang Asao became Little Huan's mommy, for which Third Master Zhu was responsible. Little Huan clung to Wang Asao's sleeve on the way to her new home.

The insects in the hills set up a never-ending racket. Wang Asao wiped her runny nose as her cheeks quivered uncontrollably. She was so skinny that if it hadn't been for her protruding belly she would have looked like a rail-thin dragon. The comparison was enhanced by her claw-like hands, which had become all bony after a lifetime of planting and weeding. The sorrow in her heart was like starch, which congealed into a mass that grew heavy and solid. She said what was in her heart:

"Sister Wang, do you think there's any chance for me to live on? Yesterday out in the field Landlord Zhang kicked me. That beast, he kicked me so hard I almost passed out. Why do you think he did that? It's easy for someone in good health to start working at the crack of dawn, but with my belly as big as it is, it's just too much for me. At noontime he found me sitting on the ground off to the side trying to catch my breath, so he came over and kicked me."

She stopped to wipe her runny nose then continued:

"Everyone knows that this baby's father has only been dead three months — it was right during the Dragon Boat Festival (May of the lunar calendar) — and I was four months pregnant. The baby's due any day now. Hai! What sort of baby is it gonna be? It'll be born with a grudge — it's daddy died at the hands of Landlord Zhang, and I just know that the same thing'll happen to me. No one can escape the clutches of a landlord."

Sister Wang patted her sympathetically, shifted her body slightly, and commented:

"Yo! You've had a tough life! How can anyone expect you to work the fields in your condition?"

Wang Asao's shoulders convulsed as she was wracked with sobs. Sister Wang's heart was pounding as she was overcome with remorse. That's what she was beginning to feel — remorse.

"Just listen to me talk! I should be doing everything possible to lessen your grief, and all I do is make you feel even worse!"

She then changed her tone of voice:

"That's what life is all about — you're busy, I'm busy, and the end result is death. Sooner or later, that's what it comes to."

She took out a hankie and dried Wang Asao's tears — a lifetime of tears, a never-ending flow.

"Elder Sister, you can't give up now. You shouldn't be so down in the dumps in your condition. Besides, give some thought to Little Huan. She's such a clever little girl that whenever you mope around or cry, she follows your lead and does the same. Here, let me make you something to eat. Just look at the sun — it's nearly noon."

Sister Wang kept some of her thoughts to herself:

"I'm sure that kick must've disturbed the womb. That could be dangerous... it could even kill the baby...."

She took the lid off the rice barrel — it was empty.

She decided to go over to Landlord Zhang's and get some rice, but just as she picked up a small bowl from the top of the barrel, Wang Asao said with a sigh:

"Don't go over there! I can just see the looks on their faces. Tell Little Huan to go over to Third Master Zhu's place on the hill behind us and borrow a little rice."

So Little Huan took the earthenware bowl and headed up the slope, her little braid swishing back and forth across her neck as she made her way to the other side of the hill. The insects making their homes in the withered wildflowers set up a din that had a withered quality to it.

3

Three months earlier, as Big Brother Wang was driving the nightsoil cart, the horse had stumbled on a rock and broken its leg. For this Landlord Zhang had docked him a year's pay. This so angered Big Brother Wang that he had taken to drinking all day long and staying out all night, stopping only to sleep in neighbors' haystacks. Eventually he had gone stark-raving mad, beating children and dogs whenever they got in his way, and running crazily through the fields shouting and cursing like a madman. Landlord Zhang had waited until the other man was sleeping in one of the haystacks, then had had one of his henchmen set fire to it. Big Brother Wang had thrashed about in the blazing haystack — Landlord Zhang's blazing haystack — his tongue thrust out as he emitted a stream of inhuman cries.

But who was there to save him? For a poor man, even his own wife belongs to someone else. All the time that Wang Asao's husband was burning to death in the front village, she had been picking potatoes in the field.

By the time she had rushed over to the still-burning haystack, her husband's bones were already cracking in the intense heat. His limbs were separated from his body, his skull looked like a broken gourd. Eventually the fire died out, but by then the smell of Big Brother Wang's burning flesh had permeated the entire village.

One of the onlookers had rubbed his eyes and uttered:

"What a way to go!"

Someone else had commented:

"I say good riddance. Now we won't have to worry about our kids' being beaten to death by that lunatic!"

Wang Asao had begun picking up Big Brother Wang's bones and wrapping them up in her wide sleeves. Holding onto them tightly, she had let out a long, piercing wail. This mournful sound had spread across the grasslands, found its way through stately old trees in the woods, and continued travelling all the way to the distant hills, where it produced an echo.

This blood-curdling wail had brought tears to the

eyes of every single woman who had gathered to watch. It had evoked in each of them the image that it was her husband who had burned to death, not Wang Asao's husband.

Some of them had forcibly loosened Wang Asao's grip on the bones she was holding, causing them to drop to the ground.

"Don't carry on like that, Wang Asao," they had urged her. "What good are those bones gonna do you? Think about what you're going to do now...."

But Wang Asao had ignored them — in fact, she hadn't even heard them. She had only herself. Like a crazed woman, she had retrieved the bones and held them tightly in her sleeves, oblivious to the fact that these bones were devoid of a soul, were devoid of flesh — her powers of discrimination had left her completely. She had begun rolling around in the stench left behind by Big Brother Wang's corpse, and had bored herself completely into the pall of grief and pain that surrounded her.

Her face streaked with tears, Little Huan had looked up at Wang Asao and said:

"Mommy, please don't cry, you'll go crazy. Look what happened to Daddy when he went crazy — he was burned to death!"

But Little Huan's plea had fallen on deaf ears, for Wang Asao had held her stomach and cried for all she was worth. She had ripped at her own clothing with her fingers and bit down hard on her own lips. She had been like a roaring lion.

After a while, Landlord Zhang had made an appearance; looking like a sinister hawk that was flapping its wings, he strode over from the front village, flyswatter in hand, eyes bulging, snorting through his nose, and literally reeking of airs of superiority. In a repressive tone of voice he had addressed Wang Asao:

"Since it's nearly dark, isn't it about time you knocked off that crying? A lunatic is dead, so what? Just what do you think his bones are worth? Go on home and start making plans for the future. I'll have some of my men bury him on Westridge."

Then he had turned to the men standing around and ordered them:

"That stench... the sooner the better!..."

The women had huddled together and whispered to one another:

"Master Zhang is always so compassionate. He's there to help, no matter what happens."

They had been unaware — completely unaware — that Master Zhang had been the man responsible for Big Brother Wang's death. The wheat stalks in the fields had undulated as though rain-swept, smoke from kitchen chimneys had hung over the roofs of all the homes in the area.

Landlord Zhang had turned and strode back to the front village, waving his flyswatter like a wand that could drain the blood from the villagers' bodies.

The impoverished village men, all of whom were as badly off as Big Brother Wang had been, had shrugged their broad shoulders and carried Big Brother Wang's bones over to Westridge.

4

Three days passed. Then five. Wang Asao was nowhere to be seen in the fields. As the women picked potatoes and cut down the grass they talked about nothing else:

"She's in such bad shape! She sure can't work with her belly that big!"

"She hasn't come out for five days now, ever since Landlord Zhang kicked her. The baby's probably already come. I'll go over tonight and see."

"If you want my opinion, I think she just gave up after Big Brother Wang's death. All she ever does is cry, and lately it's gotten even worse. Like the other day, when she was out picking potatoes as tears streamed down her face."

One of the women commented with a frown:

"That's right, there were more tears than potatoes."

Another chimed in:

"You said it! Every potato Wang Asao picked was paid for with a tear."

As their emotions climbed, a woman who was picking potatoes with one hand and cradling her child with the other said:

"We ought to all go over to her house tonight and see what's up. She's one of us, you know!"

All ten or so of the women voiced their agreement.

Uh-oh! There came Landlord Zhang! The women all lowered their heads and went back to work. He walked off and they raised their heads once again; the entire scene was reminiscent of stalks of wheat bent over by a gust of wind — the moment the wind has passed, the tips of the stalks spring back to their original position. The women picked up where they had left off:

"You couldn't expect her not to grieve. Big Brother Wang died without leaving her a single thing. Before you know it, winter will be here. We still have our menfolk, and we might not even have time to get our winter clothing ready. What about her? If she has her baby, how's she gonna take care of it? I've got it all figured out: the offspring of the rich are children; the offspring of the poor are nothing but the seeds of evil!"

"Everyone knows that! I heard that Wang Asao had three children, but that they all died."

Two of the group were widows themselves, one young and one old. Their thoughts were of themselves: the old woman was remembering how her husband had been crushed by a cart, the young one was recalling how her husband had coughed up blood before he died. These two women were the only ones who hadn't joined in on the discussion.

Here comes Landlord Zhang again! Once again the women's heads bowed low, like so many sunflowers.

Just then Little Huan's shouts could be heard in the field — they drifted above the women's heads:

"Quick...come quick! My mommy can't...can't, can't talk...."

She was a butterfly at the mercy of the wind. Not knowing which way to go, she fluttered her wings frantically and spasmodically. Tears gathered in her eyes, sloshing around like pools of quicksilver. She was holding onto her braid for dear life, stamping her feet, and wailing:

"My mommy.... What's wrong with her?... She doesn't say anything...can't talk...."

5

By the time the village women had reached Wang Asao's hut and had crowded into her room, Wang Asao was lying on the *kang*, her final labored wails filling the small room. Her body was covered with her own blood, and there in the midst of all that blood a tiny, brand-new creature was fighting for its own life.

Wang Asao's eyes looked like two large, shiny pearls — bright but unmoving. Her gaping mouth sent shivers down the women's spines — it looked like the mouth of an ape, with its teeth protruding outward.

Some of the women burst into tears, some of them shied away from the sight and moved over by the window. The room was an utter mess: brooms, water pitchers, and tattered shoes cluttered the floor. The neighbor's kitten was cowering on the window ledge, while Little Huan huddled in the corner, head down, weeping silently.

That was how Wang Asao died. Five minutes later her newly born child followed her in death.

6

As the moon's rays threaded through the trees in the woods, the coffin was borne over to Westridge in the company of a chorus of wails and sobs. Every woman in the village was present. They shuffled along, each of them dressed in rags to show to the world that they were Wang Asao's class equals.

Third Master Zhu walked in front, holding Little Huan by the hand. From off in the distance came the howls of frightened dogs. Little Huan was no longer crying; she had become a spiritual ward of the others, and the sorrow in her heart had been parcelled out to the women in the cortege. She let herself be led along the road, stepping solemnly on the shadows cast by nearby trees.

Wang Asao's coffin was carried into the Westridge woods, where the men were digging her grave.

Little Huan, that tiny spirit, had fallen asleep at the foot of a tree, the moon's rays dancing across her face. Her arms were folded around her knees, her head cradled in her hands. Her little braid was tossed lightly by the wind — she was a child born to the life of a wanderer.

Bathed in the rays of the moon, the coffin was lowered into the ground. The people began scurrying about, just like they did when a job was finished.

Third Master Zhu walked over and gently mussed Little Huan's hair:

"Wake up, child, it's time to go home."

Her eyes still closed, she muttered:

"Mommy, I'm cold."

"It's time to go home," Third Master Zhu repeated. "Your mommy's gone. You poor little thing, you're talking in your sleep."

She woke up. Then it dawned on her that tonight she wouldn't be able to go to sleep in her mommy's arms. There in the woods, underneath the moon, in front of her mother's grave, she began to roll on the ground and bawl like a baby.

"Mommy ... you don't want ... me anymore ... who am I gonna, gonna, gonna sleep ... sleep with?

"Do I ... hafta go back to ... Landlord ... Landlord Zhang's home and let them beat me?" She bit her lip and cried and cried.

"Mommy! Come home ... home with me!"

All the surrounding area was rent by the cries of this

little girl — there was an exchange of sound between the rustling leaves and the crying child. Like everyone else who witnessed this scene, Third Master Zhu was wiping the tears from his eyes.

Big Brother Wang and Wang Asao slept on in their graves in the woods.

Dogs in villages far and near kept up a howl throughout the night.

The Bridge

IN the summer and fall the water that collects under the bridge is level with the sides of the ditch.

"Huang Liangzi, Huang Liangzi, the baby's crying!"

Late at night or early in the morning these were the shouts that came from the head of the bridge. As time went on, the people who lived at the bridgehead became well acquainted with the sound and grew accustomed to hearing it.

"Huang Liangzi, the baby's hungry! Huang Liangzi ... Huang Liang ... zi."

Especially on rainy evenings or on a windy morning, in the midst of a solemn quiet, this sound echoed off the water under the bridge and was reinforced by the gusting wind as it carried into distant homes.

"Huang ... Liangzi. Huang ... Liang ... zi," sounding just like the refrain of a song.

The moon had completely disappeared below the horizon, leaving but one lonely star hanging there in the western sky. Huang Liangzi emerged from the open field east of the bridge.

Huang Liang was her husband's name, but from the day she became a wet nurse, someone had added the diminutive "zi" onto Huang Liang, and that was her new name.

"Eh? Is he already hungry so early? And after such a late feeding last night!"

During the first few days, she had had to run up to the bridge, where she looked across to the western side at the person who had come to call her; she caused the dilapidated old railings to tremble slightly, her voice seeming to swirl above the water below as she shouted:

"So early! Huh?"

But that soon changed. The phrase "Huang Liangzi" was like a code, for as soon as it reached her ears she quickly left, following the strains of the sound.

In the first blurred moments after being awakened, while her breathing was still somewhat labored, she walked, almost ran, northward along the edge of the ditch. She stopped at the first gate on the western side and fidgeted with her mussed-up hair.

— What's this? The gate's still closed ? How can that be?

"Open up! Open up!" She bent over and, with her face nearly touching the ground, peered in through the crack at the bottom of the gate. She could see the big white dog sleeping inside the courtyard.

Her head was bent down so low that the buildings beyond the gate seemed to spin round and round, the doors, the windows, everything swirling heavenward.

"Open up! Open up!"

— What's going on! Was I hearing things? No... someone was yelling, I know I heard it... I'm sure... I'm sure of it....

Nevertheless, there was nothing to do but return home; on her way back she met no one on either side of the bridge. She had yelled until the perspiration along her spine had turned cool.

— It couldn't be more than a hundred steps, maybe

eighty or so... make it two hundred... but still I have to walk around the long way, a good half mile!

Her initial plan had been to cross over by supporting herself on the railings. But the bridge no longer had any footing at all: the only things that thieves had left behind were the two railings. If only the railings too had disappeared, she would have felt easier, for then she could have taken comfort in the fact that the ditch was a natural obstacle, one which man was powerless to conquer.

...Isn't that so? Just add a couple of planks and it would be crossable... it only needs a couple of planks... this bridge, this bridge... separated only by a bridge....

She stood there beside the bridge for a moment and reflected.

— Shall I head south or north? Oh well, it's all the same, so I guess I'll go north.

The thatched hut that was her home was directly opposite the bridge. She saw the paper strips on the door fluttering in the wind and imagined herself able to simply stretch out her arm and touch the top of the small mound of earth. As she walked north alongside the ditch she glided past the small mound of earth opposite her; eventually, after she had gone a quarter of a mile up to the end of the ditch, she turned and headed back.

— Who's that calling me? Where are those shouts coming from?

Her hair was again falling in her face, so as she walked she fussed with it.

"Huang Liangzi, Huang Liangzi...." Just like before, it sounded as though someone were calling her.

"Huang . . . gua, qie . . . zi* . . . Huang . . . gua, qie . . . zi. . . ." A vegetable peddler met Huang Liangzi walking up the road.

"Huanggua, qiezi, huang . . . gua, qiezi. . . ."

An embarrassed smile adorned Huang Liangzi's face. She smiled in the direction of the vegetable peddler.

The bristlegrass atop the master's wall were getting plump, while on the eastern side of the bridge, the crying sounds of Huang Liangzi's child grew louder as they carried over to the west side of the bridge.

> Strolling, strolling . . . push our little angel to the top of the span.
> Atop the bridge catch a great butterfly;
> Mama sits down to rest by and by.
> Strolling, strolling . . . push our little angel to the top of the bridge.

Huang Liangzi no longer propped the baby carriage up against the elm tree and dozed, as she had done in the summertime, even though the sun's rays were still warm and the autumn skies were much more pleasant than the summer skies.

In his carriage with its creaky wheels the little master slept, with his white and delicate moon face, a frosty white cap neatly arranged on his head just above the eyebrows, and a lovely, spotlessly clean set of clothes covering his body.

Huang Liangzi felt uneasy, her heart began to stir as if shaken like a small bell:

"Must you cry? Don't cry now. . . . Daddy'll take you

---

* Cucumbers, eggplants. The similarity in sound between these words and her own name has confused Huang Liangzi.

in his arms and hop and run around...." Daddy was holding him now, standing on the opposite side of the bridge — her own child, pale and drawn, with a tinge of blue around the eyes and a neck just a bit too long, looking something like the withered branch of a tree. Nonetheless, Huang Liangzi felt that he was cuter than the child in the carriage. But in what way? His laughs were about the same as his cries, and when he cried he never shed big, bright tears. Even more disturbing was his apparent lack of love for his mama, now standing on the other side of the bridge; he never clapped his hands when he saw her, nor flailed his legs as he lay cradled in his daddy's arms.

And yet she felt that he was cuter than the child in the carriage, though she couldn't have told you why.

> Strolling, strolling... push our little angel to the top of the bridge.
> Strolling, strolling... push our little angel to the top of the bridge.

As she recited this to her little master she omitted the two middle lines:

> Atop the span catch a great butterfly;
> Mama sits down to rest by and by.

Since there was no spiritual bond here, they weren't really necessary.

> Strolling, strolling... to the top of the bridge, to the top of the bridge....

Gradually the song died in her throat. She paid no attention to whether or not the child enjoyed this little ditty. As she walked away from the bridgehead, with the carriage wheels making their creaking noise, she sang as before:

> To the top of the bridge,
> To the top of the bridge. . . .

"Hey! Wipe his runny nose! It's running into his mouth. What's wrong, are you blind? *Ai*! *Ai*!"

Huang Liangzi had completely forgotten that she was standing on this side of the bridge. She was beside herself with exasperation. Then, when she stretched out her arm, she nearly broke into tears and her anxieties caused her face to redden all over.

"Daddy . . . Daddy's a hopeless case — useless! But this bridge . . . this bridge . . . if only this bridge didn't separate us. . . ."

The resonance caused by the water under the bridge produced a hollow ring to Huang Liangzi's voice; her reflection quivered.

"Carry him over here! Don't just stand there and watch him cry! Come around over here. For a man it's no strain at all. Me, I have to push a baby carriage!"

The reflection of three people and a baby carriage floated on the surface of the water, but one could not tell who was standing to the east and who was standing to the west.

From that day on, "the bridge" seemed to shorten Huang Liangzi's life. Yet, to her it seemed that the sun hung up in the sky the day long without ever setting. Were the days longer, or were they shorter? She didn't know. Was the weather colder, or was it warmer? She didn't know that either. She had changed into a lined jacket, but one could attach little significance to that, for when others put on warmer clothing, she mechanically followed their lead.

As she swept up the fallen leaves by the side of the road she continued to rock the baby carriage with its creaky wheels.

The bristlegrass atop the master's wall were devoid of moisture — it had all dried up — and there were just a scant few blades still rustling in the wind. But the child's cries coming from the eastern side of the bridge had not abated a bit. Carried by the wind, they drifted over to the master's house and directly to Huang Liangzi's ears, where they were magnified in much the same way as the wings of a fly appear enormous under a microscope.

She took hunks of steamed dough, biscuits, and sometimes even stuffed dumplings and nameless, greasy-smelling snacks, and tossed them from the western side of the bridge over to the eastern side.

— Separated only by a bridge... otherwise... couldn't he be eating these things any time he wanted? You poor little devil, in your destiny there should have been a bridge!

Every time some of the food fell into the water she said to her child on the eastern side:

"You poor little devil, in your destiny there should have been a bridge."

The master never did see her tossing things over to the eastern side of the bridge, but whenever a ripple spread across the surface of the water it frightened her as much as if she were seeing a reflection of her own heart in a mirror.

— It's obvious that these things are stolen... God knows it too.

With the blue sky and white clouds reflected on the surface of the water, she felt a closeness between herself and the sky; there it was, right beneath her hand as she tossed the food across the water.

One day she managed to get several kinds of snacks — mooncakes, pears, and even some meat dumplings left over from breakfast. These were not gifts, but things she had wrapped up when the master wasn't looking.

She pushed the baby carriage ahead of her, then stood at the bridgehead, having put the snacks inside the carriage's toy compartment.

"Daddy... Daddy... Huang Liang, Huang Liang!"

But there was no one, only two stray dogs making a ruckus behind the little mound of earth. The door was closed; evidently, they were both asleep.

She decided to cross over to the eastern side. As she hurried along, pushing the carriage ahead of her, she jolted the baby's head around, but what she feared most was the creaking of the wheels.

— Where am I going? Pushing the carriage at a run... what am I doing pushing the carriage at a run... what am I running for... what am I running for? Where am I running to?

It was just as if the mistress were behind her shouting:

— Stop where you are! Stop where you are!

She so frightened herself that she broke into a sweat, her heart nearly leaping into her throat.

The child had begun to cry from being jolted around, so she tried to distract him:

"Look! Here comes a tiger!"

She woke the child sleeping on the *kang*, then watched

him grab the snacks she had brought for him. In her heart she began to feel a strange kind of happiness every time the child picked up a pear or took two or three grapes and squashed them.

"*Aiya*! That's food you're playing with — don't ruin it! What a waste of good food ... don't you even know how to eat? Here, let Mama feed you. Open up, open up. Hey! They're sour! Look at your face. They're so sour your eyes are just a couple of slits ... here, eat this mooncake. A-year-old child should be able to eat just about anything ... here, eat it ... this isn't the first meal you've ever had!"

She smiled. Invariably she felt that this child who so loved to cry and who never really laughed was somehow cuter than the one inside the carriage.

Walking back to the western side of the bridge, her mind was completely at ease. As she headed north alongside the ditch she spotted a tiny purple chrysanthemum growing on the bank. Her spirits soaring, she reached out and picked it to stick in her hair.

"Little angel. *Aiya*! What do you think of this?" She waved the flower in her hand and called to the little one, the words coming straight from her heart. Calling out to him was the only way she could express her momentary feelings of happiness. A great weight had been lifted from her heart, and for the first time she felt that her little master was as cute as her own child. She gave his cheek a friendly pinch as the carriage wheels creaked along the uneven road. She happened to notice the reflection of the carriage in the ditch water, which reminded her that she had crossed over to the eastern side of the bridge. She grew uneasy. The reflection of the carriage moved along at a quickened pace, began to flicker.

— Only a hundred and eighty steps ... still I have to go nearly half a mile out of my way. I can look at the bridge but I can't cross it.

— Huang Liangzi, Huang Liangzi! Where have you pushed that child to? — It was as though her mistress were already calling her: — what did you steal to take home? Do you hear me, Huang Liangzi!

Her own name was dancing in her head.

Without having full control of the carriage, she pushed it recklessly along the bank of the ditch, and occasionally she came so close to the ditch that the carriage nearly tumbled down into the water. Only two of its wheels were touching the ground and the child was on the verge of bouncing out. Before she reached the far end of the ditch, one of the wheels flew off and spun into the water as if thrown with great force.

Huang Liangzi stopped and looked around her; the railings on the bridge could still be seen, however indistinctly.

— That bridge! Isn't it all on account of that bridge?

She felt like crying, but her chest merely heaved twice, and that was it.

— I'm still on the eastern side of the bridge, so I'd better hurry over to the western side. She gave the carriage a push on its three wheels and maneuvered it from the eastern to the western side of the ditch.

— How am I going to explain this? I could say I was strolling by the ditch and a wheel just came off. Or should I say I was catching butterflies? But there aren't any butterflies at this time of year. Well, I could say I was catching dragonflies.... Oh, that's stupid! Anyway, now the carriage is here on the western side of the bridge, and as far as I'm concerned, it never was on the eastern side!

"Huang Liang, Huang Liang..." She had put everything out of her mind; she appeared calm and unafraid.

"Huang Liang, Huang Liang..." She pushed the baby carriage on its three wheels alongside the ditch up to the bridge and called out for her husband.

By the time the wheel was in Huang Liangzi's hand, her husband was covered to the waist with filthy mud. She pushed the carriage on its three wheels up to the master's gate, her hair hanging down and streaking her pale face.

— Here's the wheel. It fell off... it just fell off and rolled into the ditch....

She leaned against one of the gate panels and wept. The railings on that bridge with no footing, over there to the east, seemed to be watching her cry.

In the summer of the second year the shouts of "Huang Liangzi, Huang Liangzi" reverberated from the bridgehead as always. Before the sun had risen it sounded exactly like the crowing of roosters.

By the third year the calls of "Huang Liangzi" coming from the bridgehead ceased; like the quivering bridge railings, they had been obliterated. Huang Liangzi had by then moved into the master's house.

During the month of March, construction on a new bridge had begun, and by summertime, carts, horses, and pedestrians were already crossing the new bridge.

When Huang Liangzi looked out at the red lacquered railings they seemed to her fresher than any summer-blooming flowers she had ever seen before.

"Run! Come on and run! Ah, this child of ours!" Every time she saw him running across the bridge from the east, no matter how far away he was, or whether he could hear or not — however faint her voice may have been, she always said:

"Run! Come on and run! Such a great, wide bridge!"

Every day he crossed the bridge several times, carried or dragged along by his daddy. A grumbling sound emanated from the level bridge, which turned into a creaking noise whenever someone stamped his foot on it.

The bristlegrass atop the wall around the master's house was once again plump and flourishing. There was also some bristlegrass growing at the base of the wall, along with other varieties of grasses — wild opium poppies, sparrow-reed grass, and some grasses whose names are not commonly known.

Huang Liangzi picked the sparrow-reed grass to make flute-whistles, giving one each to the skinny and to the stocky child. The two of them went over to the base of the wall and picked the grass, so much of it that her lap overflowed with it. Then they went and picked the wild opium poppies.

"Bzzz, bzzz, bzzz, bzzz!" Under the elm tree in the courtyard they clamored, laughing and playing their flute-whistles.

The sounds of the child's weeping at the bridgehead were no longer heard. There, at his mama's knee, the boy laughed and sang.

One of the children was always standing in front of Huang Liangzi; to her they were both cute, and occasionally, when they pretended to be crying, she would put one on each knee.

As time went on, Huang Liangzi forgot about "the

bridge"; even though on occasion she would cross it, she took no special notice that she was on a bridge. She felt that it was as commonplace as walking along a highway — there was no difference at all.

One day Huang Liangzi discovered two gashes on her child's hands.

"Go on! Go home with your daddy and take a nap, then come back." Sometimes she dragged him across the bridge herself.

After that incident, the child would stand there at her knee, dispiritedly, often weeping, and occasionally displaying scars on his face.

"That kind of roughneck behavior isn't allowed! What's the big idea, huh... what's the big idea?" Beyond the wall or on the street or, for that matter, wherever there was no one around to see, Huang Liangzi would grab the little master's wooden spear away from him. He would then fall to the ground, crying and scolding, and sometimes would go over and hit Huang Liangzi with a toy or with a dirt clod.

"Mom, I want one of those too...."

The little master was eating meat dumplings, holding one in each hand, the oil oozing out and giving a sheen to his hand. The fragrance from the dumplings seemed to fill Little Liangzi's nostrils, no matter how far away he stood.

"Mom, I want one too... I want one...."

"What do you want? Little Liangzi, you shouldn't be begging for things... haven't you any shame? Such a greedy little mouth! You thick-skinned thing, you!"

Whenever the little master ate fruit, he cocked his head and slowly rolled his dark, round eyes. As for Little Liangzi, when he saw the other boy eating, he would suck on a leaf or stick a piece of bark on his tongue, rolling it around in his mouth and sucking at it with the tip of his tongue.

Every time the little master ate apricots, he crisply spat the pit of one onto the ground and started in on another one. The pockets of his apron would be stuffed with large, yellow apricots.

"Nice little boy. Give one to Little Liangzi... wouldn't that be nice?..." Huang Liangzi reached out and touched his pocket, but the child drew back and ran some distance away, then threw a couple of apricots to the ground.

"Go ahead, eat them! Little Liangzi, you little gremlin...." Huang Liangzi glanced at her son.

As Little Liangzi ate the apricots, the pits caused his teeth to smack against his mouth resoundingly. He always sucked on the pits for a long, long time. Afterwards, he went over and picked up the pits that the other, better-fed, child had spat out onto the ground.

One day Huang Liangzi saw her child stick his hand into a mud puddle and feel around. At the first swat from his mama he fell to the ground, then stuck both hands into the mud hole and yelled:

"Mom! The apricot pit.... I've dropped the apricot pit...."

Huang Liangzi often took her child across the bridge.

"Huang Liang! Huang Liang! Take him home with you.... Huang Liang! Tell him to stop running across the bridge...."

Now and then, at dusk or at noontime, Huang Liang's name carried from the bridgehead into people's homes. Seemingly, the strains of the "Huang Liangzi" melody were coming to life again.

"Huang Liang, Huang Liang! Take this little gremlin and tie him up! He crossed the bridge again...."

On the morning that Little Liangzi split the little master's lip, Huang Liang's whole family was involved in an uproar at the bridgehead. Huang Liangzi was shouting, Little Liangzi was running and screaming:

"Daddy... Daddy.... *Ai!*... *Ai!*..."

By that evening Little Liangzi also had a bloodied lip. An earlier wound, which had been caused by the little master, was bleeding again, but this time it was Little Liangzi's own mama who had done it.

She wiped the little master's wound clean, but both she and her husband left the wound on her own child untended.

Huang Liangzi carried her things back home with her from the west side of the bridge.

One would have thought that a sickness prevailed in her home — it was quiet, muted, the front gate seemingly never opened the day long. No smoke rose from the chimney.

The loneliness extended all the way to the bridgehead, and the families in the vicinity were deprived of their mid-summer melodics. The sounds of "Huang Liang, Huang Liang, Little Liangzi" were no longer heard.

The water under the bridge quietly flowed on. Neither Huang Liangzi's reflection nor her voice was in evidence either above or below the bridge.

By the time Huang Liangzi was summoned anew to work at the master's house, it was late fall or early winter, when the rain falling on the road had already begun to freeze into shimmering ice buds.

The ditch, on the other hand, had not frozen over, and the railings of the bridge were, as always, red.

Pausing at the bridgehead, she observed that the ditch that stretched horizontally in front of her had neither lengthened in a southerly direction nor visibly shortened to the north. To the west the housetops were, as ever, enveloped in a gray pall, which also swallowed up the gates and the courtyard walls. The withered and yellowing bristlegrass atop the walls rustled in the wind just as it had in the late fall of the year before.

But the bridge, she suddenly felt, had grown taller! It was as though climbing onto it was beyond her ability. A sort of weakness and fear gripped her.

— Ah, if only this bridge weren't here! If it weren't for this bridge, Little Liangzi couldn't run across to the western side. With it, there's nothing to stop him. It's all the fault of this bridge.

She longed for the old bridge, though as she pictured it in her mind she recalled the unpleasant emotions trying to cross it had engendered.

Little Liangzi never once crossed over to the western side while his daddy stood at the bridgehead, his arms spread wide. Whether he laughed or cried, Little Liangzi was always stopped from crossing the bridge, and whenever his runny nose got out of control, his daddy picked him up and warmed his frozen earlobes with the palms of his hands. On those occasions a long human shadow spread out across the open field on the eastern side of the bridge.

Occasionally, at dusk or perhaps when the child had fallen asleep in his daddy's arms, the long shadow of a curved back would gradually disappear. The open field on the eastern side of the bridge would be completely deserted. Yet the flicker of a lamp shining from the mound of earth in the open field remained; from time to time, the crackling noise of burning fuel emerged from within the mound of earth.

Little Liangzi lifted his dinner bowl up to his mouth as the night closed in on him from the bridgehead. The deep colors of night were like a huge curtain falling from the bridgehead up to the front of Little Liangzi's door.

On the following day Little Liangzi ran up to the bridge, as usual.

"I'm going to go find Mama... eat dumplings... she has dumplings.... Mama has some.... Mama has some sweets...." All the while, he was running and shouting, his hair blown up and back as he ran against the wind. He caught sight of his daddy's large hand catching up to him. Shouts of "Mama!" and the sounds of crying could be heard coming from the bridgehead. Carried by the wind and aided by the resonant echo from the water under the bridge, his cries entered homes far off in the distance.

Peace came to the head of the bridge on the day of the last rainfall of the year.

From that time on Little Liangzi was no more.

It was wintertime. Both sides of the bridge were snowbound, and the red railings had disappeared under the falling snow. Pedestrians, carts, and horses trod the bridge, going to the eastern and to the western sides.

That day Huang Liangzi heard her child fall into the ditch, and she ran frantically down to the water's edge. When she saw that he was no longer breathing, after having been dragged up to the bank of the ditch, she stood up and looked over the heads of the bystanders in the direction of the bridge.

Those quivering bridge railings, those red bridge railings; in her confusion she thought she saw two sets of bridge railings.

Then her chest heaved and expanded. This time she really cried.

Hands

NEVER had any of us in the school seen hands the likes of hers before: blue, black, and even showing a touch of purple, the discoloring ran from her finger tips all the way to her wrists.

We called her "The Freak" the first few days she was here. After class we always crowded around her, but not one of us had ever asked her about her hands.

Try though we might, when our teacher took roll call, we just could not keep from bursting out laughing:

"Li Jie!"

"Present."

"Zhang Chufang!"

"Present."

"Xu Guizhen!"

"Present."

One after another in rapid, orderly fashion, we stood up as our names were called, then sat back down. But when it came to Wang Yaming's turn, the process lengthened considerably.

"Hey, Wang Yaming! She's calling your name!" One of us often had to prod her before she finally stood up, her blackened hands hanging stiffly at her sides, her shoulders dropping: Staring at the ceiling, she would answer: "Pre-se-nt!"

No matter how the rest of us laughed at her, she would never lose her composure, but merely push her chair back noisily with a solemn air and sit down after what seemed like several moments. Once, at the beginning of English class, our English teacher was laughing so hard she had to remove her glasses and wipe her eyes.

"Next time you need not answer *hay-er*," she commented. "Just say 'present' in Chinese."

We were all laughing and scuffling our feet on the floor. But on the following day in English class, when Wang Yaming's name was called we were once again treated to sounds of "*Hay-er, hay-er*".

"Have you ever studied English before?" the English teacher asked as she adjusted her glasses slightly.

"You mean the language they speak in England? Sure, I've studied some, from the pockmarked teacher. Let's see, I know that they write with a *pun-sell* or a *pun*, but I never heard *hay-er* before."

"'Here' simply means 'present'. It's pronounced 'here', 'h-e-r-e'."

"*She-er, she-er*." And so she began saying *she-er*. Her quaint pronunciation made everyone in the room laugh so hard we literally shook. All, that is, except Wang Yaming, who sat down very calmly and opened her book with her blackened hands. Then she began reading in a very soft voice: "*Who-at . . . deez . . . ah-ar . . .*"*

During math class she read her formulas the same way she read essays: "$2x + y = \ldots x_m = \ldots$"

At the lunch table, as she reached out to grab a *mantou*** with a blackened hand, she was still oc-

---

* "What . . . these . . . are. . . ."
** Chinese steamed bread.

cupied with her geography lesson: "Mexico produces silver.... Yunnan... hmm, Yunnan produces marble."

At night she hid herself in the lavatory and studied her lessons, and at the crack of dawn she could be found sitting at the foot of the stairs. Wherever there was the slightest glimmer of light, that's where I usually found her. One morning during a heavy snowfall, when the trees outside the window were covered with a velvety layer of white, I thought I spotted someone sleeping on the ledge of the window at the far end of the corridor in our dormitory.

"Who's there? It's so cold there!" The slapping of my shoes on the wooden floor produced a hollow sound. Since it was a Sunday morning, there was a pronounced stillness throughout the school; some of the girls were getting ready to go out, while others were still in bed asleep. Even before I had drawn up next to her I noticed the pages of the open book on her lap turning over in the wind. "Who do we have here? How can anybody be studying so hard on a Sunday!" Just as I was about to wake the girl up a pair of blackened hands suddenly caught my eye. "Wang Yaming! Hey, come on, wake up now!" This was the first time I had ever called her name, and it gave me a strange, awkward feeling.

"*Haw-haw*... I must have fallen asleep!" Every time she spoke she prefaced her remarks with a dull-witted laugh.

"*Who-at... deez... yoou... ai*,"* she began to read before she had even found her place in the book.

"*Who-at... deez...* this English is sure hard. It's

---

* "What... these... you... I."

nothing like our Chinese characters with radicals and the like. No, all it has is a lot of squiggles, like a bunch of worms crawling around in my brain, getting me more confused all the time, until I can't remember any more. Our English teacher says it isn't hard — not hard, she says. Well, maybe not for the rest of you. But me, I'm stupid; we country folk just aren't as quick-witted as the rest of you. And my father's even worse off than me. He said that when he was young he only learned one character — our surname Wang — and he couldn't even remember that one for more than a few minutes. *Yoou . . . ai . . . yoou . . . ah-ar. . . .*" Finishing what she had to say, she tacked on a series of unrelated words from her lesson.

The ventilator on the wall whirred in the wind, as snowflakes were blown in through the window, where they stuck and turned into beads of ice. Her eyes were all bloodshot; like her blackened hands, they were greedily striving for a goal that was forever just beyond reach. In the corners of rooms or any place where even a glimmer of light remained, we saw her, looking very much like a mouse gnawing away at something.

The first time her father came to visit her he said she had gained weight: "I'll be damned, you've put on a few pounds. The chow here must be better'n it is at home, ain't that right? You keep working hard! You study here for three years or so, and even though you won't turn into a sage, at least you'll know a little somethin' about the world."

For a solid week after his visit we had a great time mimicking him. The second time he came she asked him for a pair of gloves.

"Here, you can have this pair of mine! Since you're

studyin' your lessons so hard, you oughta at least have a pair of gloves. Here, don't you worry none about it. If you want some gloves, then go ahead and wear these. It's comin' on spring now, and I don't go out much anyway. Little Ming, we'll just buy another pair next winter, won't we, Little Ming?" He was standing in the doorway of the reception room bellowing, and a crowd of his daughter's classmates had gathered around him. He continued calling out "Little Ming this" and "Little Ming that", then gave her some news from home: "Third Sister went visitin' over to Second Auntie's and stayed for two or three days! Our little pig has been gettin' a couple extra handfuls of beans every day, and he's so fat now you've never seen the like. His ears are standin' straight up. Your elder sister came home and pickled two more jars of scallions."

He was talking so much he had worked up a sweat, and just then the school principal threaded her way through the crowd of onlookers and walked up to him: "Won't you please come into the reception room and have a seat?"

"No thanks, there's no need for that, that'll just waste everyone's time. Besides, I couldn't if I wanted to; I have to go catch a train back home. All those kids at home, I don't feel right leavin' 'em there." He took his cap off and held it in his hands, then he nodded to the principal. Steam rose from his head as he pushed the door open and strode out, looking as though he had been chased off by the principal. But he stopped in his tracks and turned around, then began removing his gloves.

"Daddy, you keep them. I don't need to wear gloves anyway."

Her father's hands were also discolored, but they were both bigger and blacker than Wang Yaming's.

Later, when we were in the reading room, Wang Yaming asked me: "Tell me, is it true? If someone goes into the reception room to sit and chat, does it cost him anything?"

"Cost anything! For what?"

"Not so loud; if the others hear you, they'll start laughing at me again. She placed the palm of her hand on the newspaper I was reading and continued: "My father said so. He said there was a teapot and some cups in the reception room, and that if he went inside the custodian would probably pour tea, and that he would have to pay for it. I said he wasn't expected to, but he wouldn't believe me, and he said that even in a small teahouse, if you went in and just had a cup of water you'd have to pay something. It was even more likely in a school, he said. 'Just think how big a school is!'"

The principal said to her, as she had several times in the past: "Can't you wash those hands of yours clean? Use a little more soap! Wash them good and hard with hot water. During morning calisthenics out on the playground there are several hundred white hands up in the air — all but yours; no, yours are special, very special!" The principal reached out her bloodless, fossil-like transparent fingers and touched Wang Yaming's blackened hands. Holding her breath somewhat fearfully, she looked as though she were reaching out to pick up a dead crow. "They're a lot less stained than they used to be — I can even see the skin on the palms now. They're much better than they were when you first got here — they were like hands of iron then!

Are you keeping up with your lessons? I want you to work a little harder, and from now on you don't have to take part in morning calisthenics. Our school wall is low, and there are a lot of foreigners strolling by on spring days who stop to take a look. You can join in again when the discoloring on your hands is all gone!" This lecture by the school principal was to bring an end to her morning calisthenics.

"I already asked my father for a pair of gloves. No one would notice them if I had gloves on, would they?" She opened up her bookbag and took out the gloves her father had given her.

The principal laughed so hard at this she fell into a fit of coughing. Her pallid face suddenly reddened: "What possible good would that do? What we want is uniformity, and even if you wore gloves you still wouldn't be like the others."

The snow atop the artificial hill had melted, the bell being rung by the school custodian produced a crisper sound than usual, sprouts began to appear on the willow trees in front of the window, and a layer of steam rose from the playground under the rays of the sun. As morning calisthenics began, the sound of the exercise leader's whistle carried far into the distance; its echo reverberated among the households in the clump of trees outside the windows. We ran and jumped like a flock of noisy birds, intoxicated by the sweet fragrance that drifted over from the new buds on the branches of the trees. Our spirits, which had been imprisoned by the winter weather, were set free anew, like cotton wadding that has just been released.

As the morning calisthenics period was coming to an end we suddenly heard someone calling to us from an upstairs window in a voice that seemed to be floating up to the sky: "Just feel how warm the sun is! Aren't you hot down there? Aren't you...."

There standing in the window behind the budding willows was Wang Yaming.

By the time the trees were covered with green leaves and were casting their shade all over the compound, a change had come over Wang Yaming — she had begun to languish and black circles had appeared around her eyes. Her ears seemed less full than before and her strong shoulders began to slump. On one of the rare occasions when I saw her under one of the shade trees I noticed her slightly hollow chest and was reminded of someone suffering from consumption.

"The principal says my schoolwork's lagging behind, and she's right, of course; if it hasn't improved by the end of the year, well.... *Haw-haw!* Do you think she'll really keep me back a year?" Even though her speech was still punctuated with that *haw-haw*, I could see that she was trying to hide her hands — she kept the left one behind her back, while all I could see of the right one was a lump under the sleeve of her jacket.

We had never seen her cry before, but one gusty day when the branches of the trees outside the windows were bending in the wind, she stood there with her back to the classroom and to the rest of us and wept to the wind outside. This occurred after a group of visitors had departed, and she stood there wiping the tears from her eyes with darkened hands that had already lost a good deal of their color.

"Are you crying? How dare you cry! Why didn't you go away and hide when all the visitors were here? Just look at yourself. You're the only 'special case' in the whole group! Even if I were to forget for the moment those two blue hands of yours, just look at your uniform — it's almost gray! Everybody else has on a blue blouse, but you, you're special. It doesn't look good to have someone wearing clothes so old that the color has faded. We can't let our system of uniforms go out the window because of you alone." With her lips opening and closing, the principal reached out with her pale white fingers and clutched at Wang Yaming's collar: "I told you to go downstairs and not come back up until after the visitors had left! Who told you to stand out there in the corridor? Did you really think they wouldn't see you out there? And to top it all, you had on this pair of oversized gloves."

As she mentioned the word "gloves" the principal kicked the glove that had dropped to the floor with the shiny toe of her patent shoe and said: "I suppose you figured everything would be just fine if you stood out there wearing a pair of gloves, didn't you? What kind of nonsense is that?" She kicked the glove again, but this time, looking at that huge glove, which was large enough for a carter to wear, she couldn't suppress a chuckle.

How Wang Yaming cried that time; she was still weeping even after the sounds of the wind had died down.

She returned to the school after summer vacation. The late summer weather was as cool and brisk as autumn, and the setting sun turned the cobbled road a deep red. We had gathered beneath the crab-apple tree by the school entrance and were eating crab-apples when a horsecart from Mount Lama carrying Wang Yaming rumbled up. In the silence following the arrival of the cart her father began taking her luggage down for her, while she held onto her small washbasin and a few odds and ends. We didn't immediately make way for her when she reached the step of the gate. Some of us called out to her: "So here you are! You've come back!" Others just stood there gaping at her. As her father followed her up to the steps, the white towel which hung from his waistband flapping to and fro, someone said: "What's this! After spending a summer at home, her hands are as black as they were before. Don't they look like they're made of iron?"

I didn't really pay much attention to her ironlike hands until our post-autumn moving day. Although I was half asleep, I could hear some quarreling in the next room:

"I don't want her. I won't have my bed next to hers!"

"I don't want mine next to hers either."

I tried listening more attentively, but I couldn't hear clearly what was going on. All I could hear was some muffled laughter and an occasional sound of commotion. But going out into the corridor that night to get a drink of water, I saw someone sleeping on one of the benches. I recognized her at once — it was Wang Yaming. Her face was covered with those two blackened hands, and her quilt had slid down so that half was on the ground and the other half barely covered her legs. I thought that she was getting in some studying by the corridor light, but I saw no books beside her. There was only a clutter of personal belongings and odds and ends on the floor all around her.

On the next day the principal, followed closely by Wang Yaming, made her way among the neatly arranged beds, snorting as she did so and testing the freshly tucked bedsheets with her delicate fingers.

"Why, here's a row of seven beds with only eight girls sleeping on them; some of the others have nine girls sleeping in six beds!" As she said this she took one of the quilts and moved it slightly to one side, telling Wang Yaming to place her bedding there.

Wang Yaming opened up her bedding and whistled contentedly as she made up the bed. This was the first time I had ever heard anyone whistle in a girls' school. After she made up the bed she sat on it, her mouth open and her chin tilted slightly higher than usual, as though she were calmed by a feeling of repose and a sense of contentment. The principal had already turned and gone downstairs, and was perhaps by then out of the dormitory altogether and on her way home. But the old housemother with lackluster hair kept shuffling back and forth, scraping her shoes on the floor.

"As far as I'm concerned," she said, "this won't do at all. It's unsanitary. Who wants to be with her, with those vermin all over her body?" As she took a few steps toward the corner of the room, she seemed to be staring straight at me: "Take a look at that bedding! Have a sniff at it! You can smell the odor two feet away. Just imagine how ludicrous it is to have to sleep next to her! Who knows, those vermin of hers might hop all over anyone next to her. Look at this, have you ever seen cotton wadding as filthy as that!"

The housemother often told us stories about how she had accompanied her husband when he went overseas to study in Japan, and how she should be considered an overseas student also. When asked by some of the girls: "What did you study?" she would respond: "Why study any particular subject? I picked up some Japanese and noticed some Japanese customs while I was there. Isn't that studying abroad?" Her speech was forever dotted with terms like "unsanitary", "ludicrous", "filthy" and so on, and she always called lice "vermin".

"If someone's filthy the hands show it." When she said the word "filthy" she shrugged her broad shoulders, as though she had been struck by a blast of cold air, then suddenly darted outside.

"This kind of student! Really, the principal shouldn't have...." Even after the lights-out bell had sounded the housemother could still be heard talking with some of the girls in the corridor.

On the third night Wang Yaming, bundle in hand and carrying her bedding, was again walking along behind the white-faced principal.

"We don't want her. We already have enough girls here."

They started yelling before the principal had even laid a finger on their bedding, and the same thing happened when she moved on to the next row of beds.

"We're too crowded here already! Do you expect us to take any more? Nine girls on six beds; how are we supposed to take any more?"

"One, two, three, four..." the principal counted. "Not enough; you can still add one more. There should be six girls for every four beds, but you only have five. Come on over here, Wang Yaming!"

"No, my sister's coming tomorrow, and we're saving that space for her," one of the girls said as she ran over and held her bedding in place.

Eventually the principal led her over to another dormitory.

"She's got lice, I'm not going to sleep next to her."

"I'm not going to either."

"Wang Yaming's bedding doesn't have a cover and she sleeps right next to the cotton wadding. If you don't believe me, just look for yourself!"

Then they began to joke about it, saying they were all afraid of Wang Yaming's black hands and didn't dare get close to her.

Finally the black-handed girl had to sleep on a bench in the corridor. On mornings when I got up early I met her there rolling up her bedding and carrying it downstairs. Sometimes I ran into her in the basement storage room. Naturally, that was always at nighttime, so as we talked I kept looking at the shadows cast on the wall; the shadows of her hands as she scratched her head were the same color as her black hair.

"Once you get used to it, you can sleep on a bench or even on the floor. After all, sleep is sleep no matter where you lie down, so what's the difference! Studying is what matters. I wonder what sort of grade Mrs Ma is going to give me in English on our next exam. If I don't score at least sixty I'll be kept back at the end of the year, won't I?"

"Don't worry about that; they won't keep you back just because of one subject," I assured her.

"But Daddy told me I only have three years to graduate in. He said he won't be able to handle the tuition for even one extra semester. But this English language — I just can't get my tongue right for it. *Haw-haw*...."

Everyone in the dormitory was disgusted with her, even though she was sleeping in the corridor, because she was always coughing during the night. Another reason was that she had begun to dye her socks and blouses right in the dormitory.

"When clothes get old, if you dye them they're as good as new. Like, if you take a summer uniform and dye it gray, then you can use it as an autumn uniform. You can dye a pair of white socks black, then...."

"Why don't you just buy a pair of black socks?" I asked her.

"You mean those sold in the stores? When they dye them they use too much alum, so not only don't they hold up, but they tear as soon as you put them on. It's a lot better to dye them yourself. Socks are so expensive it just won't do to throw them away as soon as they have holes in them."

One Saturday night some of the girls cooked some eggs in a small iron pot, something they did nearly every Saturday, as they wanted to have something special to eat. I saw the eggs they cooked this time when they took them out of the pot. They were black, looking to me as if they had been poisoned or something. The girl who carried the eggs in roared so loudly her glasses nearly fell off: "All right, who did it! Who? Who did this!?"

Wang Yaming looked over at the girl as she squeezed her way through the others into the kitchen. After a few *haw-haw* she said: "It was me. I didn't know anyone was going to use this pot, so I dyed two pairs of socks in it. *Haw-haw* ... I'll go and...."

"You'll go and do what?"

"I'll go and wash it."

"You think we'd cook eggs in the same pot you used to dye your stinky old socks! Who wants it?" The iron pot was hurled to the floor, where it clanged in front of us. Scowling, the girl wearing glasses then flung the blackened eggs to the floor as though she were throwing stones.

After everyone else had left the scene, Wang Yaming picked the eggs up off the floor, saying to herself: "Hm! Why throw a perfectly good iron pot away just because I dyed a couple of pairs of socks in it? Besides, how could new socks be 'stinky'?"

On snowy winter nights the path from the school to our dormitories was completely covered by a blanket of snow. We just pushed on ahead as best we could, bumping our way along, and when we ran into a strong wind we either turned around and walked backwards or walked sideways against the wind and snow. In the mornings we had to set out again from our dormitories, and in December it got so bad that our feet were numb with the cold, even if we ran. All of this caused a lot of grumbling and complaining, and some of the girls even began calling the principal names for placing the dormitories so far from the school and for making us leave for school before dawn.

Sometimes I met Wang Yaming as I was walking alone. There would be a sparkle to the sky and the distant snow cover as we walked along together, the moon casting our shadows ahead of us. There would be no other people in sight as the wind whistled through the trees by the side of the road and windows creaked and groaned under the driving snow. Our voices had harsh sounds to them as we talked in the sub-zero weather until our lips turned as stiff and numb as our legs and we stopped talking altogether, at which time we could hear only the crunching of the snow beneath our feet.

When we rang the bell at the gate our legs were so cold they felt like they were about to fall off, and our knees were about to buckle under us.

One morning — I forget just when it was — I walked out of the dormitory with a novel I wanted to read tucked under my arm, then turned around and pulled the door shut tight behind me. I felt very ill at ease as I looked at the blurred houses off in the distance and heard the sound of the shifting snow behind me; I grew more frightened with every step. The stars gave off only a glimmer of light, and the moon either had already set or was covered by the gray, dirty-looking clouds in the sky. Every step I took seemed to add another step to the distance I had yet to go. I hoped I would meet someone along the way, but dreaded it at the same time; for on a moonless night you could hear the footsteps long before you saw anyone, until the figure suddenly appeared without warning before you.

When I reached the stone steps of the school gate my heart was pounding and I rang the door bell with a trembling hand. Just then I heard someone on the steps behind me.

"Who is it? Who's there?"

"Me! It's me."

"Were you walking behind me all the time?" It gave me quite a fright, because I hadn't heard any steps but my own on the way over.

"No, I wasn't walking behind you; I've already been here a long time. The custodian won't open the door for me. I don't know how long I've been here shouting for him."

"Didn't you ring the bell?"

"It didn't do any good, *haw-haw*. The custodian

turned on the light and came to the door, then he looked out through the window. But he wouldn't open the door for me."

The light inside came on and the door opened noisily, accompanied by some angry scolding: "What's the idea of shouting at the gate at all hours of the night! You're going to wind up at the bottom of the class anyway, so why worry about it?"

"What's going on! What's that you're saying?" Before I had even finished, the custodian's manner changed completely.

"Oh, Miss Xiao, have you been waiting there long?"

Wang Yaming and I walked to the basement together; she was coughing and her face, which had grown pale and wrinkled, shivered for a few moments. With tears induced by the cold wind on her cheeks, she sat down and opened her school book.

"Why wouldn't the custodian open the door for you?" I asked.

"Who knows? He said I was too early. He told me to go on back, saying that he was only following the principal's orders."

"How long were you waiting out there?"

"Not too long. Only a short while... a short while. I guess about as long as it takes to eat a meal. *Haw-haw*."

She no longer studied her lessons as she had when she first arrived. Her voice was much softer now and she just muttered to herself. Her swaying shoulders slumped forward and were much narrower than they had been, while her back was no longer straight and her chest had grown hollow. I read my novel, but very softly so as not to disturb her. This was the first time I had been so considerate, and I wondered why it was only the first time. She asked me what novels I had read and whether I knew *The Romance of the Three Kingdoms*. Every once in a while she picked the book up and looked at its cover or flipped through the pages. "You and the others are so smart. You don't even have to look at your lessons and you're still not the least bit worried about exams. But not me. Sometimes I feel like taking a break and reading something else for a change, but that just doesn't work with me."

One Sunday, when the dormitory was deserted, I was reading aloud the passage in Sinclair's *The Jungle* where the young girl laborer Marija had collapsed in the snow. I gazed out at the snow-covered ground outside the window and was moved by the scene. Wang Yaming was standing right behind me, though I was unaware of it.

"Would you lend me one of the books you've already read? This snowy weather depresses me. I don't have any family around here, and there's nothing to shop for out on the street — besides, everything costs money."

"Your father hasn't been to see you for a long time, has he?" I thought she might be feeling a little homesick.

"How could he come? A round trip on the train costs two dollars, and then there'd be nobody at home."

I handed her my copy of *The Jungle*, since I had read it before.

She laughed — "*haw-haw*" — then patted the edge of the bed a couple of times and began examining the cover of the book. After she walked out of the room, I could hear her in the corridor reading the first sentence of the book loudly just as I had been doing.

One day sometime after that — again I forget just

when it was, but it must have been another holiday — the dormitory was deserted all day long, right up to the time that moonlight streamed in through the windows, and the whole place was extremely lonely. I heard a rustling sound from the end of the bed, as though someone were there groping around for something. Raising my head to take a look, I noticed Wang Yaming's blackened hands in the moonlight. She was placing the book she had borrowed beside me.

"Did you like it?" I asked her. "How was it?"

At first she didn't answer me; then, covering her face with her hands and trembling, she said: "Fine."

Her voice was quivering. I sat up in bed, but she moved away, her face still buried in hands as black as the hair on her head. The long corridor was completely deserted, and my eyes were fixed on the cracks in the wooden floor, which were illuminated by moonlight.

"Marija is a very real person to me. You don't think she died after she collapsed in the snow, do you? She couldn't have died. Could she? The doctor knew she didn't have any money, though, so he wouldn't treat her ... *haw-haw*." Her high-pitched laugh brought tears to her eyes. "I went for a doctor once myself, when my mother was sick, but do you think he would come? First he wanted travel money, but I told him all our money was at home. I begged him to come with me then, because she was in a bad way. Do you think he would agree to come with me? He just stood there in the courtyard and asked me: 'What does your family do? You're dyers, aren't you?' I don't know why, but as soon as I told him we were dyers he turned and walked back inside. I waited for a while, but he didn't come back out, so I knocked on his door again. He said to me through the door: 'I won't be able to take care of your mother, now just go away!' So I went back home." She wiped her eyes again, then continued:

"From then on I had to take care of my two younger brothers and two younger sisters. Daddy used to dye the black and blue things, and my elder sister dyed the red ones. Then in the winter of the year that my elder sister was engaged her future mother-in-law came in from the countryside to stay with us. The moment she saw my elder sister she cried out: 'My God, those are the hands of a murderess!' After that, Daddy no longer let anyone dye only red things or only blue things. My hands are black, but if you look closely you can see traces of purple; my two younger sisters' hands are the same."

"Aren't your younger sisters in school?"

"No. Later on I'll teach them their lessons. Except that I don't know how well I'm doing myself, and if I don't do well then I won't even be able to face my younger sisters. The most we can earn for dyeing a bolt of cloth is thirty cents. How many bolts do you think we get a month? One article of clothing is a dime — big or small — and nearly everyone sends us overcoats. Take away the cost for fuel and for the dyes, and you can see what I mean. In order to pay my tuition they had to save every penny, even going without salt, so how could I even think of not doing my lessons? How could I?" She reached out and touched the book again.

My gaze was still fixed on the cracks in the floor, thinking to myself that her tears were much nobler than my sympathy.

One morning just before our winter holiday Wang Yaming was occupied with putting her personal belongings in order. Her luggage was already firmly bound, standing at the base of the wall. Not a soul went over to say goodbye to her. As we walked out of the dormitory, one by one, and passed by the bench which had served as Wang Yaming's bed, she smiled at each of us, at the same time casting glances through the window off into the distance. We scuffled along down the corridor, then walked downstairs and across the courtyard. As we reached the gate at the fence, Wang Yaming caught up with us, panting hard through her widely opened mouth.

"Since my father hasn't come yet, I might as well get in another hour's class work. Every hour counts," she announced to everyone present.

She worked up quite a sweat in this final hour of hers. She copied down every single word from the blackboard during the English class into a little notebook. She read them aloud as she did so and even copied down words she already knew as the teacher casually wrote them on the board. During the following hour, in geography class, she very laboriously copied down the maps the teacher had drawn on the board. She acted as though everything that went through her mind on this her final day had taken on great importance, and she was determined to let none of it pass unrecorded.

When class let out I took a look at her notebook, only to discover that she had copied it all down incorrectly. Her English words had either too few or too many letters. She obviously had a very troubled heart.

Her father still hadn't come to fetch her by nightfall, so she spread her bedding out once again on the bench. She had never before gone to bed as early as she did that night, and she slept much more peacefully than usual. Her hair was spread out over the quilt, her shoulders were relaxed, and she breathed deeply; there were no books beside her that night.

The following morning her father came as the sun was fixed atop the trembling snow-laden branches of the trees and birds had just left their nest for the day. He stopped at the head of the stairs, where he removed the pair of coarse felt boots that were hanging over his shoulders, then took a white towel from around his neck and wiped the snow and ice off his beard.

"So you flunked out, did you?" Small beads of water were formed on the stairs as the ice melted.

"No. We haven't even had exams yet. The principal told me I didn't need to take them, since I couldn't pass them anyway."

Her father just stood there at the head of the stairs staring at the wall, and not even the white towel that hung from his waist was moving. Having already carried her luggage out to the head of the stairs, Wang Yaming went back to get her personal things, her washbasin, and some odds and ends. She handed the large pair of gloves back to her father.

"I don't want them, you go ahead and wear them!" With each step in his coarse felt boots, he left a muddy imprint on the wooden floor.

Since it was still early in the morning, few students were there looking on as Wang Yaming put the gloves on with a weak little laugh.

"Put on your felt boots! You've already made a mess of your schooling, now don't go and freeze your feet off too," her father said as he loosened the laces of the boots, which had been tied together.

The boots reached up past her knees. Like a carter,

she fastened a white scarf around her head. "I'll be back; I'll take my books home and study hard, then I'll be back. *Haw ... haw*," she announced to no one in particular. Then as she picked up her belongings she asked her father: "Did you leave the horsecart you hired outside the gate?"

"Horsecart? What horsecart? We're gonna walk to the station. I'll carry the luggage on my back."

Wang Yaming's felt boots made slapping noises as she walked down the stairs. Her father walked ahead of her, gripping her luggage with his discolored hands. Beneath the morning sun long quivering shadows stretched out in front of them as they walked up the steps of the gate. Watched from the window, they seemed as light and airy as their own shadows; I could still see them, but I could no longer hear the sounds of their departure. After passing through the gate they headed off into the distance, in the direction of the hazy morning sun.

The snow looked like shards of broken glass, and the further the distance, the stronger the reflection grew. I kept looking until the glare from the snowy landscape hurt my eyes.

On the Oxcart

LATE March. Clover covers the banks of the streams. In the early light of the morning our cart crushes the red and green grasses at the foot of the hill as it rumbles through the outskirts of Grandfather's village.

The carter is a distant uncle on Mother's side. He flicks his whip, but not to strike the rump of the ox; the tip merely dances back and forth in the air.

"Are you sleepy already? We've only just left the village! Drink some plum nectar now, and after we've crossed the stream ahead you can sleep." Grandfather's maid is on her way to town to visit her son.

"What stream? Didn't we just cross one?" The yellow cat we're bringing back from Grandfather's house has fallen asleep in my lap.

"The Houtang Stream."

"What Houtang Stream?" My mind is wandering. The only things from Grandfather's village still visible in the distance are the two gold balls on top of the red flagpole in front of the ancestral temple.

"Drink a cup of plum nectar, it'll perk you up." She is holding a cup of the dark yellow liquid in one hand as she puts the lid back on the bottle.

"I'm not going to need anything... perk me up? You perk yourself up!"

They both laugh as the carter suddenly cracks his whip.

"You young lady, you... you sharp-tongued little scamp... I, I...." He turns over from alongside the axle and reaches out to grab hold of my hair. Drawing my shoulders back, I clamber to the rear of the cart. Every kid in the village is scared of him. They say he used to be a soldier, and when he pinches your ear it hurts like the dickens. Sister Wuyun has gotten down off the cart to gather a lot of different kinds of flowers for me. Now the wind blowing in from the wildwood has picked up a bit, and her scarf is flapping around her head. I pretend that it's a raven or a magpie, like the ones I saw in the village. Look at 'er jumpin' up and down, just like a kid! She's back in the cart now, singing out the names of all kinds of flowers. I've never seen her so happy.

I can't tell what those low, coarse, grunting noises from the carter mean. Puffs of smoke from his short pipe float back on the wind. As we start off on our journey, our hopes and expectations are far off in the distance.

I must have fallen asleep, but I don't know if it happened before we crossed Houtang Stream, or just where it happened. I remember waking up once, and through the cobwebs of my mind I thought I saw the boy who watches over the ducks beckon to me. There was also the parting scene between me and Xiaogen as he straddled his ox. And I could see Grandfather again taking me by the hand and saying, "When you get home tell your granddad to come on over during the cool autumn season and visit the countryside... you tell him that your old Grandpa's quail and his best *gaoliang* wine are waiting here for him to enjoy with me together... you tell him that I can't get around so well anymore; otherwise these past couple of years I would have gone...."

The hollow sound of the wheels wakes me up. The first thing I see is the yellow ox plodding along the road. The carter isn't sitting there by the axle where he should be — there he is, behind the cart. Instead of the whip, he's holding a pipe in his hand. He keeps stroking his chin with his other hand; he is staring off into the horizon. Sister Wuyun is stroking the yellow cat's tail in her lap. She has wrapped her blue cotton scarf around her head below her eyebrows, and the creases on her nose are easier to see than usual because of the dust that lines them.

They don't know that I'm awake.

"By the third year there were no more letters from him. You soldiers...."

"Was your husband a soldier too?" I couldn't hold back. My carter-uncle pulls me backwards by my pigtail.

"And no more letters at all after that?" he asks.

"Since you asked me, I'll tell you. It was just after the Mid-autumn Festival — I forget which year it was. I had just finished eating breakfast and was slopping the pigs in front of the house. 'Soo-ee, soo-ee!' I didn't even hear Second Mistress from the Wang family of South Village as she came running up, shouting, 'Sister Wuyun, Sister Wuyun! My mother says it's probably a letter from Brother Wuyun.' She held a letter right under my nose. 'Here, let me have it. I want to see....' I don't know why, but I felt sick at heart. Was he still alive? He.... My tears fell on the red-bordered envelope, but when I tried to wipe it dry with my hand, all I did was smudge the red border onto the white paper. I threw the slop down in the middle of the yard and went into my room to change into some clean clothes. Then I ran as fast as I could to the school in South Village to see the schoolmaster. I was laughing through my tears. 'I've got a letter here from someone far away; would you please read it to me.... I haven't had a single word from him for a year.' But after he took the letter from me and read it, he said it was for someone else. I left the letter there in the school and ran home. I didn't go back to feed the pigs or put the chickens to roost; I just went inside and lay down on the *kang*. For days I was like someone whose ghost had left her."

"And no more letters from him at all?"

"None." After unscrewing the lid from the bottle of plum nectar, she drinks a cupful, then another.

"You soldiers, you go away for two or three years, you say, but do you return home?... How many of you ever do? You send your ghosts home for us to see...."

"You mean?..." the carter blurts out. "Then he was killed in battle somewhere?"

"That's what it amounted to; not a word for more than a year."

"Well, was he killed in battle or wasn't he?" Jumping down from the cart, he grabs his whip and snaps it in the air a couple of times, making sounds like little explosions.

"What difference does it make? The bitter life of a soldier doesn't allow for much good fortune." Her wrinkled lips look like pieces of torn silk, a sure sign of a fickle nature and a life of misfortune.

As we pass Huang Village the sun begins to set and magpies are flying over the green wheat fields.

"Did you cry when you learned that Brother Wuyun

had died in battle?" As I look at her, I continue stroking the yellow cat's tail. But she ignores me and busies herself with straightening her scarf.

The carter scrambles up into the cart by holding on to the handrail and jumping in, landing right above the axle. He is about to smoke; his thick lips are sealed as tightly as the mouth of the bottle.

The flow of words from Sister Wuyun's mouth is like the gentle patter of rain; I stretch out alongside the handrail and before long I've dozed off again.

I awake to discover that the cart is stopped alongside a small village well — the ox is drinking from the well. Sister Wuyun must have been crying, because her sunken eyes are all puffed up and the crows-feet at the sides of her eyes are spread open. Scooping up a bucketful of water from the well, the carter carries it over to the cart.

"Have some — it's nice and cool."

"No, thanks," she replies.

"Go ahead and drink some. If you're not thirsty, at least use some of it to wash your face." He takes a small towel from his waistband and soaks it in the water. "Here, wipe your face. The dust has clouded your eyes."

I can't believe it, a soldier actually offering his towel to someone! That strikes me as peculiar, since the soldiers I've known only know how to fight battles, beat women and pinch children's ears.

"That winter I traveled to the year-end market where I sold pig bristles. I stood there shouting, 'Good stiff pig bristles ... fine long pig bristles. ...' By next year I had just about forgotten my husband ... didn't think about him at all. But all that did was make me mad at myself, because he might still have been alive. The following autumn I went into the fields with the others to harvest sorghum... here, look at my hands — they've seen their share of work....

"I got a more permanent job in the fields the next spring, so I took the baby with me, and the whole family was split up for two or three months. But we got back together the next winter. All kinds of ox hairs... pig bristles... even some bird feathers, we gathered them up... during the winter we gathered them all up, cleaned them, and took them into town to sell when the weather turned warm. If I could catch a ride on a cart, I took Little Baldy into town with me.

"But this time I went in alone. The weather that day was awful — it had been snowing almost every day — and the year-end market wasn't very crowded. I wouldn't have been able to sell all my pig bristles even if I'd only brought a few bundles. I squatted there in the marketplace from early morning till the sun was setting in the west. Someone had put a poster up on the wall of a large store at the intersection, which everyone stopped to read. I heard that the 'proclamation' had been put up early in the morning ... or maybe it had only been there since around noontime... some of the people read several sentences aloud as they looked at it. I didn't know what it was all about... they were saying, 'Proclamation this' and 'proclamation that', but I couldn't figure out just what was being 'proclaimed'. I only knew that a proclamation was the business of officials and had nothing to do with us common folk, so I couldn't figure out why there were so many people interested in it. Someone said it was a proclamation about the capture of some army deserters. I overheard a few other tidbits here and there... in a few days the deserters were going to be delivered to the county seat to be shot."

"What year was that? Was that the execution of twenty-odd deserters in 1921?" Absent-mindedly letting down his rolled-up sleeves, the carter rubs his cheekbone with his hand.

"How should I know what year it was... besides, execution or not, what business was it of mine? Anyway, my pig bristles weren't selling so good and things were looking bleak." Rubbing her hands together briefly, she suddenly stretches out her hand as though she were catching a mosquito.

"Someone was reading out the names of the deserters. I looked over at a man in a black gown and said to him, 'Read those names again for me!' At first I was holding the pig bristles in my hand, then I heard him say Jiang Wuyun... Jiang Wuyun... the name seemed to be echoing in my ears. After a moment or two, I felt like throwing up, like some foul-smelling thing was stuck in my throat; I wanted to swallow it... but couldn't... my eyes were burning... the people looking at the 'proclamation' crowded up in front of it, so I backed off to the side. I tried to move up again and take a look, but my legs wouldn't hold me. More and more people came to look at the 'proclamation', and I kept backing up... farther... farther...."

I can see that her forehead and the tip of her nose are beaded with perspiration.

"When I returned to the village it was already late at night. Only when I was getting down from the cart did I remember the pig bristles... they'd been the farthest thing from my mind at the time... my ears were like two chips of wood... my scarf had fallen off, maybe on the road, maybe in the city...."

Now that she has removed her scarf, we can see that her earlobes are missing.

"Just look at these; that's what it means to be a soldier's wife...."

The ends of her scarf, which she has fixed tightly over her head again, move slightly when she speaks.

"Wuyun was still alive, and I felt like going to see him; at least we could be together as husband and wife one last time....

"In February I strapped Little Baldy onto my back and went into town every day.... I heard that the 'proclamation' had been put up several more times, though I never went to see that God-awful thing again. I went to the yamen to ask around, but they only said, 'That's none of our business!' They sent me to the military garrison... ever since I was a kid I've had a fear of officials... a country girl like me. I'd never been to see one of 'em. Those sentries with their bayoneted rifles sent shivers up and down my spine. *Oh, go ahead! After all, they don't just kill people on sight.* Later on, after I'd gone to see them lots of times, I wasn't afraid any longer. After all, out of the three people in our family, they already had one of us in their clutches. They told me that the deserters hadn't been sent over yet. When I asked them when they would be, they told me, 'Wait another month or so!' But when I got back to the village I heard that the deserters had already come from some county seat or other — even today I can't remember which county seat it was, since the only thing that mattered to me was that they had been sent over — and they said if

I didn't hurry and go see him, it'd be too late. So I strapped Little Baldy onto my back and went back to town, where I asked around again at the military garrison. 'Why all the impatience?' they asked me. 'How many more hundreds of times are you going to ask? Who knows, maybe they won't be sent over at all.' One day I spotted some big official riding in a horsedrawn carriage with its bells jingling as it came out from the garrison buildings. I put Little Baldy down on the ground and ran over; luckily the carriage was heading toward me, so I knelt down in front of it.... I didn't even care if the horse trampled me.

" 'Venerable sir, my husband... Jiang Wu —' Before I even got his name out I felt a heavy blow on my shoulders... the carriage driver had pushed me over backwards. I must've been knocked over.... I crawled over to the side of the road. All I could see was that the driver was wearing a military cap.

"I stood up and strapped Little Baldy onto my back again. There was a river in front of the garrison, and for the rest of the afternoon I just sat there on the riverbank looking at the water. Some people were fishing out on the river and some women were washing clothes on the bank. Farther off, at the bend in the river, the water was much deeper, and the crests of waves passed in front of me, one after the other. I don't know how many hundreds of waves I saw passing by as I sat there. I felt like putting Little Baldy down on the riverbank and jumping straight to the bottom. Just leave that one little life behind; as soon as he started crying, someone would surely come and take him away.

"I rubbed his little chest and said something like,

'Little Baldy, you go to sleep.' Then I stroked his little round ears... those ears of his, honestly, they're so long and full, just like his daddy's. Looking at his ears, I was seeing his daddy."

A smile of motherly approval spreads across her face.

"I kept on rubbing his chest and said again, 'You go to sleep, Little Baldy.' Then I remembered that I still had a few strings of cash on me, so I decided to put them on his chest. As I reached over... reached over to put... when I was putting them on his... he opened his eyes... another sailing boat came around the riverbend, and when I heard the shouts of 'Mama' from a child on the boat, I quickly picked Little Baldy up from the sandbank and held him... against my chest...."

Her tears flow along with the motion of her hands as she tightens the scarf under her chin.

"But then... then, I knew I had to carry him back home. Even if I had to go begging, at least he would have his mother... he deserved a mother."

The corners of her blue scarf quiver with the movements of her cheekbones.

Our path is being crossed by a flock of sheep, herded by a shepherd boy playing a willow flute. The grass and the flowers in the wildwood all blend together, bathed in the slanting rays of the sun, so that all we can see is a vast jumbled patch of yellow.

The carter is now walking alongside the cart, raising trails of dust on the road with the tip of his whip.

"... it wasn't until May that the people at the garrison finally told me, 'They'll be coming soon.'

"Toward the end of the month a big steamship pulled up to the wharf in front of the garrison. God, there were a lot of people! Not that many people coming out to watch the river-lanterns on the July Fifteenth Festival."

Her sleeves are waving in the air.

"The families of the deserters were standing over to the right, so I moved over there with them. A man in a military cap came over and pinned a kind of badge on each of us.... I don't know what they said, since I can't read.

"When they were about to lower the gangplank, a troop of soldiers came up to those of us who were wearing the badges and grouped us into a circle. 'Move a little farther back from the riverbank, move a little farther....' They pushed us back some thirty or forty feet away from the steamship with their rifle butts. An old man with a white beard stood next to me, holding some packages in his hand. 'Uncle, why did you bring those things along?' I asked him. 'Huh? Oh, I have a son and a nephew ... one package for each ... when they get to the next world it wouldn't be right for them not to have clothes to wear.'

"They lowered the gangplank ... some of the people began to cry as soon as they saw the gangplank being lowered ... me, I wasn't crying. I planted my feet squarely on the ground and kept my eyes on the ship ... but no one came out. After a while, an officer wearing a foreign sword leaned over the railing and said, 'Have the families move farther back; they're going to be leaving the ship now.' As soon as they heard him bark out the order, the soldiers herded us even farther back with their rifle butts, all the way back to the beanfield by the edge of the road, until we were standing there on top of the bean shoots. The gangplank came crashing down, and out they came, led by an officer, their leg-irons clanking along. I can still see it: the first one out was a short little man... then five or six more... not one of them with broad shoulders like Little Baldy's daddy... really, they looked wretched, their arms hanging stiffly in front of them. I watched for a long time before I realized that they were all wearing manacles. The harder the people around me cried, the calmer I became. I just kept my eyes on the gangplank.... I wanted to ask Little Baldy's daddy, 'Why couldn't you just be a good soldier? Why did you have to desert? Look here at your son; how can you face him?'

"About twenty of them came down, but I couldn't spot the man I was looking for; from where I stood they all looked the same. A young wife in a green dress lost control and busted through the rifles holding us back... they weren't satisfied with just calling her back; no, they went out and grabbed her, and she started rolling in the dirt and crying out, 'He hadn't even been a soldier for three months... not even....' Two of them carried her back. Her hair was all mussed up and hanging down in her face. After about the time it takes to smoke a pipeful, they led those of us wearing badges over... the more we walked, the closer we got, and the closer we got, the harder it was for me to spot Little Baldy's daddy... my eyes started to blur... the weeping sounds around me scared me....

"Some of them had cigarettes in their mouths, some were cursing... some were even laughing. So this was the stuff soldiers are made of. I guess you could say that soldiers don't give a damn what happens to them.

"I looked them over; Little Baldy's daddy wasn't

there for sure. *That's strange*! I grabbed hold of an officer's belt: 'What about Jiang Wuyun?' 'What's he to you?' 'He's my husband.' I put Little Baldy down on the ground and he started to cry. I slapped him in the mouth, then I began hitting the officer: 'What have you done with him?'

" 'Good for you, lady, we're with you....' The prisoners were shouting from where they were crouching. When the officer saw what was happening, he quickly called some soldiers over to drag me away. 'It's not only Jiang Wuyun,' he said. 'There are a couple of others who haven't been sent over yet; they'll be over in a day or two on the next ship. Those three were the ringleaders of this group of deserters.'

"I put the child on my back and left the riverbank, with the badge still pinned on, and walked off. My legs were all rubbery. The streets were filled with people who had come over to watch the excitement. I was walking behind the garrison buildings, and there at the base of the garrison wall sat the old man with the two packages, but now he only had one left. 'Uncle, didn't your son come either?' I asked him. He just arched his back and stuck the ends of his beard into his mouth and chewed on them as he wept.

"He told me, 'Since he was one of the ringleaders, they carried out their capital punishment on the spot.' At the time I didn't know what 'capital punishment' meant...."

At this point she begins to ramble.

"Three years later, when Little Baldy was eight, I sent him to the beancurd shop ... that's what I did. I go to see him twice a year and he comes home once every two years, but then only for ten days or a couple of weeks...."

The carter has left the side of the cart and is walking along a little path, his hands clasped behind his back. With the sun off to the side, he casts a long shadow which divides with every step he takes.

"I have a family too...." The words seem to fall from his lips, as though he is speaking to the wildwood.

"Huh?" As Sister Wuyun loosens her scarf a little, the wrinkles above her nose quiver momentarily. "Really? You're out of the army, and still you don't go home?"

"What's that? Go home, you say! You mean go home with nothing but the clothes on my back?" The carter sneers as he rubs his nose hard with his coarse hand.

"Haven't you put a little something away these past few years?"

"That's exactly why I deserted, to make a little money if I could." He cinches his belt tighter.

I put on another cotton jacket and Sister Wuyun throws a blanket over her shoulders.

"Um! Still another mile to go. Now if we had a harness horse...um! We could be there in nothing flat! An ox is no good. This beast just plods along with no spirit, and it's no good at all on a battlefield."

The carter open his straw bag and takes out a padded jacket from which pieces of straw fall off and swirl in the wind. He puts it on.

The winds at dusk are just like February winds. In the rear of the cart the carter opens up the wine jug that my mother's father had given my father's father.

"Here, drink! As they say, 'In the midst of a journey open a jug of wine, for the poor love to gamble.' Now for two cups of wine." After drinking several cups, he opens his shirt and exposes his chest. He is chewing on some pieces of jerky, causing frothy bubbles to gather at the corners of his mouth. Whenever a gust of wind blows across his face, the bubbles on his lips expand a little.

As we near the town, through the gray overcast we can tell only that it is not a patch of open country, nor a mountain range, nor the seashore, nor a forest.... The closer our cart comes to the town, the more it seems to recede into the distance. The pores on our faces and hands feel sticky. Another look ahead, and this time even the end of the road is lost from view.

The carter puts the wine jug away and picks up his whip. By now the ox's horns have grown indistinct.

"Haven't you returned home or even received a letter since you left?" The carter hasn't heard her. He blows on his whistle to urge the ox on. Then he jumps down from the cart and walks along up front with the animal. An empty cart with a red lantern hanging from its axle comes rolling up to us.

"A heavy fog!"

"It sure is!"

The carters are calling out to each other.

"A heavy fog in March... that either means war or a year of drought...."

The two carts pass on the road.

The Family Outsider

I was crouching up in the tree, becoming increasingly frightened now that the sun had set. The leaves of the tree rustled around me, while all I could see of the passersby on the street was their black silhouettes. The doors and windows of the buildings in the compound were now nothing but black holes, and on top of the wall beside me a stray cat ran back and forth screeching. I slid down from the tree, and though the rear door of the house was open, I didn't dare go in until I had checked to see if Mother was asleep. As I drew up next to her window I heard the rustling of a sleeping-mat inside.

"You wretched little brat, how dare you come back here!"

I turned on my heel and slipped away along the wall that ran past the sidewing of the house, then stood for a while in the grass in the middle of the compound, for some time unaware that I had broken off some blades of grass and was chewing on them. All the insects that I knew so well during the day had stopped chirping; there were other kinds making noises now that it was nighttime, and the sounds they made were more subdued, crisper, and more prolonged. The grass I was standing in was as tall as I was, and smooth to the touch; a light melodic rustling sound fell on my ears, but so softly that I wasn't sure if I was actually hearing it or not.

"Scat, go away... always jumping and crowding around. Who wants you?"

My uncle, You Erbo, had returned, and I could hear his shouts at the dog continuing all the way to the side room of the house. I also detected the familiar slapping sounds of his shoes with their worn-down heels. Then I heard creaking sounds from the door of the side room.

"Has Ma gone to sleep?" As I parted the grass and emerged from the clump I saw that the paper window in the side room where You Erbo lived was lit up from inside as if by flames. I pushed open his door and stood in the opening.

"Aren't you in bed yet?"

"Not yet," I said.

He was standing in front of the lighted stove. Skewered on the tip of a poker was an ear of corn.

"Haven't you had dinner yet?" I asked.

"What dinner? Who would leave any dinner for me?"

"I haven't eaten either," I said.

"Haven't eaten — why not? After all, you're a member of the family." His neck was even redder than it usually was after he'd been drinking, and his bulging veins looked like the small branches burning in the stove.

"Go on now, go to bed!" I didn't really believe he was saying this to me.

"But I haven't eaten either!" I looked at the roasting corn, which was beginning to turn brown.

"So why didn't you get to eat?"

"Ma beat me."

"Beat you? Why'd she do that?"

There is a difference in the warmth felt in the hearts of adults and children; here I was on the verge of tears, and there was a trace of a smile on his lips. Still, he was the only one who seemed to be on my side — he was certainly better than Mother. I immediately began to feel some regret. I found myself standing beside him clutching some sticks of firewood, grasping them very tightly, for a long time unwilling to let them go. Since I didn't dare look him in the face, I kept my eyes fixed on his waist or on the pile of firewood at his feet, and I was moved to say:

"Erbo, the next rainy day we have I won't tease you with 'When it rains there are bubbles (on the pond), and only a turtle wears a straw hat.'"

"So your Ma beat you, did she? Well, you probably deserved it."

"Huh?" I said. "Look, she made me go without dinner!"

"Made you go without dinner. You, you do everything you're told, don't you?"

"Look, I was crouching up in the tree, and she came at me with a poker. Look here, she broke the skin on my arm." I dropped the firewood and rolled up my sleeve to show him.

"So the skin's broken. Why did she poke at you? Was there a reason or wasn't there?"

"Because I took some *mantou*."*

"And you still wonder why. You're a one! This is the first time I've seen a seven-year-old girl who's a thief already, who even steals from her own family and

---

* Chinese steamed bread.

gives the stuff away!" He removed the ear of corn from the poker. Since the fire was still burning, I could see his whiskers clearly sweeping back and forth across the ear of corn.

"I only took three — not many...."

"Um!" He glanced at me sideways and seemed about to say something, but he didn't. He just kept his whiskers moving over the corn.

"And I didn't get any dinner, either," I said, biting my fingernails.

"You didn't eat because you didn't want to. You're a member of the family!" As if throwing food to a dog, he tossed half an ear of corn at my feet.

One day I noticed my mother's head lying on her pillow with her hair all rumpled, so I knew she was fast asleep. I took the egg basket from the foot of the wooden stand and ran out to join the neighbor kids, who were all waiting for me inside the empty millshed at the rear of the compound. I moved along the wall without incident, then called out softly to the kids, who reached through the window and pulled the basket inside. One of them, who was bigger than the rest of us, and whom we all called Little Elder Brother, hunched his shoulders and gaped when he saw the eggs. The little mute girl, Yaba, showed her exceptional delight by snorting: "Ah, ah!"

"Hey, quiet down a little! Sister Hua's mother will skin her alive!"

We closed the window, then started a fire right on top of the millstone; smoke began to billow up from the burning twigs and dry grass, as rats scurried back and forth beneath the millstone. The windmill stood at a corner of the wall, its big wheel covered with spiderwebs. At the foot of the bolting frame there was a layer of powder from several kinds of grains, which in turn was covered with the dried-up carcasses of all kinds of insects.

"Now, let's divide 'em up, so many for each of us, and everybody cooks his own."

Our faces turned red as the bonfire blazed up.

"Okay, let's cook 'em! Go ahead and put 'em in... three apiece."

"But there's one left over; who gets that?"

"Ah, give it to Yaba."

She took it and went "Uh, uh."

"Quiet down, don't make so much noise! Don't mess up our chance to get something to eat!"

"Now you got an extra egg, so next time don't scold us with that sign language of yours! Huh? Yaba!"

When the eggshells began turning brown, we were so excited we almost lost our heads and started screaming.

"Hey! Hey! They're almost ready!"

"Get ready. They'll be ready to eat soon."

"My egg's bigger than anyone's, big as a duck's egg."

"Shhh, quiet down. Hua's mother is probably awake after all this."

From the other side of the window came some scraping sounds, which we immediately knew were being made by the big white dog as he scratched at the mud on the wall facing. But we also thought we heard my mother's voice. It *was* my mother calling me! Just as the eggshells were beginning to crack and split, her shouts pierced through the paper covering of the window. When she stopped, I gingerly eased myself out the window and walked along very slowly, pretending I was still half asleep; by the time I was standing right in front of her, no matter what I did I couldn't stop my heart from pounding.

"Ma, what're you calling me for?" I'm sure my face was pale and drawn.

"Just a minute." She turned and went back as if she were looking for something.

I thought she must be going to get something to hit me with, and although I felt like running away I forced myself to stand there and wait.

"Here, take this child out and play with her," she said as she handed my baby sister over to me.

I could barely hold her — I was sweating all over.

"Go on! What are you waiting for?" In fact, the noise from the millshed couldn't travel this far; Mother went over to her mirror and began combing her hair.

I walked by an oblique path to the locked door at the front of the millshed, where I told the kids: "Nothing's wrong, it's okay. Ma doesn't suspect a thing."

I was a few steps away from the door when a strange aroma rushed my way, spreading throughout the entire compound. By the time I got back to the house and put my baby sister down on the *kang*, that aroma filled the whole room.

"Which family is frying eggs, I wonder? They sure smell good." Mother's high nose reflected in the mirror gave me a fright.

"They're not frying the eggs, they're roasting them! I'm sure of it! Ha! You can smell the eggshells. I wonder who... what stupid housewife is *roasting* her eggs? You can smell them a mile away."

"Maybe it's them over at Sister Wu's," I said as

I watched the smoke coming out the window of the millshed beyond the vegetable garden. When I ran back there, though, the fire was completely out. The other kids crowded around me, nearly brushing up against my hair.

"Ma kept asking, who was roasting eggs? Who was roasting eggs? I told her it must be them over at Sister Wu's. Ha! Is this Sister Wu's? Why, it's just a pack of little devils."

We burst out laughing, then we jumped down from the millstone, but that was only the beginning; the others began chasing rats in the millshed after I told them mother had gone out to do some gossiping, taking the baby with her.

"Who's in there?" We knew at once it was You Erbo tapping on the windowsill.

"If you want to come in, just climb up," someone in the group answered him. "What are you yelling for?"

At first he couldn't see anything but just stood and waved his hands outside the window. Then he said:

"What have we here?" He sniffed the air deeply a couple of times: "Something's going on here; where's that odor coming from?" He climbed up to the windowsill, and when that short, sturdy body of his jumped in through the window, it was as if the millstone had hit the floor with a resounding thud. He took a couple of turns around the millstone, sniffing the air as he walked, the red whiskers above his upper lip twitching continually and making it look as if he had an autumn caterpillar squirming above his mouth.

"Have you been making a fire? Here, look at the ashes on the millstone. Huazi, this is your doing! If I don't tell your mother.... All day long you keep leading that bunch of wild brats into trouble." As he was about to climb back up to the window he suddenly spied the basket: "Who brought this out? Isn't this our egg basket? Huazi, you've stolen something again, haven't you? Without your mother's knowledge!"

As he picked up the basket to go, we poked fun at his straw hat, saying, "It looks like a little earthenware bowl, or a water bucket."

But that night I got a beating, after which I slunk over to one of the window ledges and licked away my tears.

"You Erbo, Tiger Yu, that good-for-nothing, crummy old man." I kept crying and muttering my contempt for him. But before long I had forgotten all about it, and I was soon back with the other kids undoing his waistband, running behind him with a staff, pushing his brimless straw hat off his head, twittering and teasing him just as we did the big white dog in the compound.

Toward the end of fall there was a long lonely spell: cold winds filled all the dark, empty buildings; the tall grasses which grew in the compound dried up and crumpled to the ground; white frost covered all the vegetable stalks in the garden behind the house; the branches of the old elm tree which stood beside the wall waved their few remaining leaves in the wind; the sky looked gray and the clouds shapeless; there was occasional drizzle and once in a while a light flurry of fine snow.

Feeling a little weary, and wanting to explore, I fixed a trunk and a cupboard as stepping blocks and climbed up into the attic space over the room where we stored our old things. It was dark up there; I experienced feelings difficult to describe. I rubbed up against a small wooden chest, picked it up, and carried it back to the opening of the attic. With the aid of the light coming in through the opening I looked at it and found it secured with a shiny little brass lock. I held it next to my ear and shook it, then tapped it with the palm of my hand — a hollow rattle sounded inside. Very disappointed to discover that I couldn't open the chest, I put it back where I had found it and moved on to a place even further in, and much darker, where I crawled around searching for something else. It was impossible to stand in the pitch black space with its uneven footing, so I just crawled around, and whenever my fingers touched something I picked it up and felt it. My hand bumped a small glass jar, which I also carried back to the spot where the light shone in, and what I found filled me with delight — the jar was full of dried black dates. I didn't waste another minute, but holding tightly to my precious find, started to climb down. However, just as the tip of my foot reached the top of the trunk I quickly snaked my body back in through the opening and remained crouched just inside the attic for some time.

There was You Erbo, trying to open up the very trunk I had used as a stepping block. After watching him work on the lock for a long time, I noticed that he was biting on something that he held in his hand. He cocked his head, and his teeth made clicking sounds; after he bit whatever it was, he gave it a twist with his fingers and tried it on the lock of the trunk. The last time he did it the brass lock gave a metallic twang, and I realized that what he had been twisting was a piece of wire. He took off his hat and tucked that little bent tool inside it.

He rummaged through the contents of the trunk a number of times; in it were some red seat cushions, a blue embroidered apron made of coarse material, some embroidered women's shoes, and a tangled ball of multicolored silk threads. Resting at the bottom of the trunk was a brass wine decanter, dark yellow. After a while he grabbed hold of the trunk with his sinewy arms and shook it.

It struck me that he was going to move the trunk away, and if he did that how was I going to get down? Several times he picked it up, but he always set it back down again, until I was on the verge of calling out to him. After a moment he took off his waistband, bent down and laid it out on the ground, and placed the seat cushions on top of it one by one, after which he tied a knot in the waistband and cinched up the cushions. Panting heavily, he tried to lift them all up. Why didn't he hurry up and get out of here? I thought of Yaba and some of the other kids, and in my mind's eye I could see them eating the things I had found, which filled me with a sense of proud delight.

"Hey there, here ... here are some nice, oily black dates." I had already thought out exactly what I wanted to say to them. Meanwhile the dates glistened in front of my eyes, all smooth and shiny, and it seemed as if they were already dancing around in my throat.

He didn't move the trunk after all, but began locking it up again. Then he stood the brass wine decanter on top of the trunk and walked off. As I stretched my body as far as I could, so that the soles of both feet were planted firmly on top of the trunk, I felt soreness in my chest where I had held the glass jar so tightly against it. You Erbo walked back in, and the first thing he did was pick up the bundle of seat cushions next to the door. Then he came over to get the brass wine decanter he had placed on top of the trunk; when he had picked it up and tucked it inside his clothes up against his belly, he noticed someone standing in the corner of the room — me. A broad grin quickly spread across his face, the likes of which I had never seen on him before — every tooth in his mouth was exposed, and his lips seemed to be spreading out as if nothing could stop them.

"You won't tell?" Large beads of sweat dotted his forehead.

"Tell what?"

"Don't tell, that's a good child." He patted my head.

"Then will you let me take this glass jar with me?"

"Go ahead!"

He wasn't even looking as I also snatched up five *mantou* from the basket next to the door and ran out.

On the day Mother said some things were missing, I was standing right beside her.

"I don't know anything about it," I said.

"That's strange. It was clearly locked; where did the key come from?" As she said this, she pointed her sharp chin belligerently at the others in the family. The young cook with the crooked neck said:

"Hmmm! Who could it have been?"

"I don't know anything about it," I said again, although in my mind the images were as clear as ever: there was You Erbo tying up the seat cushions in his waistband and putting the brass wine decanter against his belly, smack up against his skin; it almost felt as if he were inside me gnawing loudly on that piece of wire. My ears were warm and flushed, so I shut my eyes for a moment, but when I opened them again I was still looking right at that open trunk.

"I don't know anything about it," I said for the third time.

Finally I said: "I didn't see anything."

After a while Mother found a piece of wire and tried for a while to make a sort of key out of it, but was unable to bend it.

"Not like that. You have to use your teeth, like this: bite it and then give it a twist. Bite it again...." Look out! If I were to let my tongue start moving, I might blurt it all out. I realized I was already making the motions with my hands; so I kept my mouth shut tight and put my arms behind me, keeping my eyes on the others.

"This is really strange; we're not talking about little things. So how could they have been taken out of the compound? Unless it was at night, but even then a thief wouldn't have been able to get away with them." My mother's pointed chin frightened me. As she spoke she pushed on the window with her hand:

"Aha! The stuff was taken out through the front door. Look! This window hasn't been opened all summer. Look here, this slit we sealed up last fall is still intact." Then she pushed me away with her hand: "Look out, you're going to trip me. Move over!"

She took another look around the room: "You don't believe me; well, there are only a few places that stuff could have gone to, and I think I have part of the answer. If you don't believe me, we'll just see. We can't let this happen. In the spring a brass chafing pot turned up missing. Everyone said it had just been misplaced, and would be found sooner or later; or they said it might have been lent out. Whoever heard of such a thing! It was sold to pay gambling debts long ago! We treat him like a member of the family, though he still complains that we don't. All right. Before long he'll be taking the very roof beams from the house!"

"Ah, ah!" The cook took hold of his apron and wiped the corners of his mouth with it. His crooked neck looked like a bent candle wick. After Mother and the others had left I remained standing there.

At dinner that night the cook asked You Erbo: "They say you don't eat mutton, but how about sheep's intestines?"

"No, I can't eat them either," he said into his rice bowl.

"Then I should tell you, Master You, that there's a piece of sheep's intestine in these fried hot peppers."

"Why didn't you say so before? ... this ... this —" He put down his chopsticks, moved his neck, which was turning red again, and turned his head round very, very slowly, like an earthenware vase slowly being rotated.

"I'm a coarse man; all my life I've eaten everything ... except that ... I don't ... eat ... the flesh of ... a sheep ... don't wear ... sheepskin hats ... don't wear ... sheepskin ... clothes. ..." He drew out each word in a slow monotone as he continued:

"Next time, Yang An, I'm telling you, whatever you're cooking — I don't care if you're frying vegetables or just making soup — if there's any sheep's ... um, let me know first. I'm not that greedy an eater! I don't mind what I eat. Even plain pickled vegetables are all right, so long as I can be spared anything from the body of a sheep!"

"But Master You, let me ask you something: what sort of wine decanter do you use when you drink wine? Does it have to be a brass one?" Yang An's chin was raised high in the air.

"Aren't all wine decanters the same?" He put his chopsticks down again, picked up the pewter decanter beside him and rapped it on the table a couple of times. "What about this one? It's a pewter decanter, but it's the wine I drink; and the taste of the wine has nothing to do with the decanter... humph! And it's not... when I was young I always liked this pewter decanter... polished it up all nice and shiny."

"Tell me, Master You, how are brass wine decanters?"

"Nothing wrong with them, since they can be polished brighter than any other kind."

"Right, brass decanters are the best after all. Ha, ha-ha." The cook started laughing, and as he was filling my rice bowl he laughed so hard he nearly dropped it.

Mother bit a hot pepper and blew out sharply to cool her tongue, so that several grains of rice landed on my hand.

"Humph! Yang An, you're laughing at me because I don't eat mutton, but I really can't eat it. You see, when I was only three months old I lost my mother. I was raised on sheep's milk, and if I hadn't been, how could I have lived these sixty-odd years?"

Yang An slapped his knee. "You're really a man of conscience; you've never done anything to anyone in bad conscience, have you? Say, Master You —"

"You young people, you don't believe in this, and that's no good. A man has to keep in mind where he came from; he can't turn his back on the past and repay kindness with evil — a man has to repay kindness with kindness. You'll find that in all the stories that are told. For example, a sheep took the place of my mother; if not... if not, could I have lived these sixty-odd years?" He straightened his back and pushed away the plate of fried hot peppers and sheep's intestine with his chopsticks.

After dinner he left the table, his brimless straw hat clutched in his hand, and walked off along the brick path, the heels of his shoes dragging along behind the toes. His feet looked like two pieces of grimy wood, and steam seemed to be rising from the cooking-pot shape that was his head.

Mother joined the cook in a hearty laugh: "A brass wine decanter, aha! And some seat cushions... you ask him whether he knows anything about them." The scar on Yang An's neck seemed larger than usual to me.

I was a little frightened of my mother; she picked up a fat drumstick with that bony hand of hers and raised it to her mouth, exposing all her teeth as she tore off a piece of meat.

On another occasion when Mother beat me, I ran to the tree and climbed up it, but since there were hardly any leaves on the branches to shield me, the little stones that Mother was hurling struck painfully all over my body, like sharp awls.

"If you climb any higher... if you climb *any* higher, I'll get a long pole and drag you down from there!"

The tree trunk around which my arms were tightly

wrapped seemed to shudder slightly as she said that; by then I had already reached the top of the tree and was about to climb out onto one of the branches.

"You little monkey, you little monster, I'll fix you one of these days!" She paced back and forth under the tree and did not throw stones at me for some time.

It had been several days since I last climbed the tree, and experienced a strange sensation; as I looked out all around me it seemed that I was higher than everything else in the world. The people and carts out on the road, neighboring buildings, all were below me; I was even level with the pole holding the bean-sprout seller's sign over on the back road.

"You wretched little brat, are you going to come down from there or not?" Mother said "wretched little brat" so often it was just my name. "Well? Yes or no?" As long as she couldn't get her hands on me, I wasn't all that frightened of her.

At a moment when she was off guard, I jumped from the tree to the top of the wall. "Ha! Now look where I am!"

"That's a good child; are you going to climb the pole in front of the Temple of the Patriarch next?" It was not my mother who answered me, but someone standing on the other side of the wall.

"Hurry and get down from there before you cave in the top of that wall. I'll go tell your mother to come give you a beating." It was You Erbo.

"I can't come down. You see, look over there. Ma's over at the base of the tree waiting for me."

"What for?" He walked in through the wooden gate.

"She's going to beat me!"

"Beat you for what?"

" 'Cause I wet my pants."

"How disgusting! You ought to be ashamed of yourself, a seven-year-old girl still wetting her pants. Are you coming down or not? You're caving in the wall!" He was snorting like a pig.

"Grab her and pull her down; today I'm going to show her just who I am!"

As Mother said this, You Erbo began rolling up his trousers.

"What's he doing?" I thought to myself.

"All right! Little Huazi, now you're going to see where your antics will get you. Just you wait."

As I watched him climb up into the lowest fork of the tree, I was on the verge of tears and my throat seemed to expand.

"I'm going to ... I'm going to tell ... I'm going to tell...."

Mother didn't seem to understand what I was saying, but You Erbo stopped where he was and remained crouching there at the large fork in the tree.

"Come on down, that's a good child; nothing's going to happen. Your mother won't hit you; hurry down from there. Tomorrow after breakfast I'll take you to the park so you won't be around the house, where you'd wind up getting beaten." He put his arms around me and carried me down from the top of the wall to the tree, and from there to the ground. I rubbed the tears away as I heard him say:

"That's a good child; tomorrow we'll go to the park."

The next morning I waited for him at the main gate, but when he did walk toward me there was no talk of, "Come on, let's go!" So I chased after him, tugging on his belt when I caught up.

"Didn't you say you were going to take me to the park today?"

"What are you talking about? What park? You go on and play, go on now!" He kept his eyes straight ahead as he walked, not even glancing at me. It was as though what was said yesterday had come from someone else's mouth. I just hung onto his belt, so he twisted his body as if he were shaking off some kind of insect, trying to get free of me.

"Then I'll tell, I'll tell that the brass wine decanter...."

He glanced around him, then said with a sigh: "Well, shall we go, you little blackmailer?"

He didn't look at me once as we were walking, nor did he give a second's thought to how captivated I was by a little rubber man in one of the shop windows. I couldn't even look at it too long, for by the time I turned my head back, he had walked a long ways down the road. When he got to the little wooden bridge at the entrance to the park, I ran past him.

"Here we are! We're here!" I was so happy I spread my arms out wide and felt as if I could fly.

The bare trees and cool arbors were all there before me beckoning. The minute I walked through the entrance my ears were assailed with the sounds of cymbals and drums coming from a circus, an almost deafening din that nearly made me lose my sense of direction. I was leading You Erbo along by the little round gourd on his tobacco pouch. As we passed by a white canvas tent I heard some voices inside:

"Are you afraid?"

"Nope."

"You've got the nerve to do it?"

"I've got the nerve."

I didn't know where You Erbo was headed.

We had already passed by vaudeville shows, Western peep-shows, monkey acts, dancing bears, and puppet shows; from that point on there wasn't a thing left to be seen. The layer of leaves on the ground got thicker until the path under our feet was completely covered. "Erbo, aren't we going to watch the circus?" I let go of the little round gourd on his tobacco pouch and moved away from him a little, watching the expression on his face: "They have a tiger in there; I've seen it, but I've never seen the elephant. Somebody said this circus has three elephants, a big one and two small ones. The big one ... the big one ... well, somebody said that his trunk — just his trunk alone — is longer than the poker we use for the fire at home." His expression didn't change at all. I ran from his left side over to his right, and back again to his left: "Is that right? You Erbo, is that right, huh? Did you ever see it?" Since I was walking backwards all this time, I tripped over an exposed tree root and fell to the ground.

"Watch where you're going!" He didn't move to help me, so I picked myself up.

At the far end of the park there was a little tea shop, where I figured he was heading because he was thirsty. But he didn't enter the tea shop; instead he went around to the rear where there was a small shed made of grass mats. He took me in with him, and although it was very dark inside, I could see a man at the far end making some gestures and striking something made of bamboo. As soon as You Erbo entered he moved over to one side and sat on a long bench, while I stood just in front of him. Even after I'd been standing there so long my legs were growing numb I still had no idea what that man was doing. He was wearing a pigtail, just like a girl, and he stuck out one leg like a shadow boxer, drew it back, then pushed out one hand; he kept it up as he walked around in a circle, after which, *Bang!* he struck the piece of bamboo. It didn't look like a Chinese opera performance, nor a monkey show, but more like the routine of a patent-medicine peddler, though no one was buying any patent medicine.

I soon grew tired of watching what was happening in front of me, so I began looking around — there wasn't another child in the place. As soon as a vacant spot opened up on the bench in front, You Erbo led me up there, where we both sat down, though I couldn't stop fidgeting for thinking of that elephant.

"Erbo, let's go and see that elephant, okay? Let's not watch this."

"Quiet down," he said. "Just sit there and listen."

"Listen to what? What is it?"

"He's telling the story from *Romance of the Three Kingdoms* where Guan Gong kills Cai Yang."

"What's a Guan Gong?"

"Guan Laoye. Haven't you ever been to the Guan Laoye Temple?"

Then it came to me: in the Guan Laoye Temple, he was the one riding a red horse.

"Oh yeah! Guan Laoye rides a red —"

"Just listen." He cut me off.

I listened for a while, but still didn't understand anything, so I turned around and sat facing the rear, where I saw a blind man whose eyes were coated with white film, and a man with only one leg who was holding a cane in his hands. The man sitting next to me had his arm wrapped in a cloth sling fastened around his neck. When the sounds *Bang! Bang! Bang!* resounded from the piece of bamboo, I noticed tears running down You Erbo's face.

I was determined to see the elephant, so on our way back I stopped in front of the white tent and refused to walk any further.

"If you want to see it, wait until after lunch. We can come back." You Erbo walked slowly away from me: "Let's go home and eat lunch, then we can come back and see it."

"No! I'm not going to eat, I'm not hungry. I'll go home after I've seen it." I tugged on his tobacco pouch.

"They won't let just anyone go in, you have to buy a ticket. Can't you see that doorkeeper standing over there?"

"Then what's to stop us from buying a ticket?"

"Where's the money going to come from? Two people's tickets would cost several dozens of strings of cash."

"I noticed that you had some money — didn't you just give some to that man in the tent?" I was clinging to his body.

"I only gave him a few coppers! That's all I had; there's no more."

"I don't believe you; I saw a whole lot!" I stood on tiptoe and felt around in his lapels and even poked my fingers into the inside pockets.

"You see, that's all there is! I don't have any more, and I have no way to make money. There's just enough to gamble a little once a month or so; sometimes I win a little, but I also lose a lot of the time. Um-hmm." He looked down at the five or six coppers I held in my hand.

"Now do you believe me, child? I simply don't have any more, and won't have. . . ." He kept talking as we crossed the wooden bridge, while the clamor and noise from the circus troupe followed us as we walked. There was a lottery stand on the other side of the bridge surrounded by a bunch of kids. You Erbo laid down a couple of coppers for me, so I pulled a slip of paper from the wire loop, and when I dipped it in the bowl of water a bright red "5" suddenly appeared.

"What number is it?"

"Can't you see? It's a '5'!" I nudged him with my elbow.

"How could I tell? I can't read a word, since I never spent a single day in school."

On the road home I ate all five of the candy balls I had won.

The next time I saw You Erbo steal something must have been during the following summer, since the purslane flowers were a fiery red, and the tall grasses in the compound, which grew much faster than I, rose above my head; bees, dragonflies, and other kinds of insects that I didn't recognize were there in profusion. There was another special kind of grass on which light purple flowers bloomed, row after row standing there so tall that the buds looked like countless little flags waving atop the grassy field.

After lunch I waited for some friends to come over, but not a single one showed up. So I ran over to the grain storeroom, where I had seen Mother go in with a large platter early in the morning. "Hah!" I thought, there must be something of interest on that platter. She had hidden it skillfully; instead of placing it in the rice cupboard or in one of the huge grain bins, she had hung it by a rope from the rafters. As I was looking at that intriguing platter I heard what sounded like mice scurrying around inside one of the bins, either there or inside the wall. Whatever it was, I could hear scuffling noises, then after a while some panting sounds — could it be a weasel? Somewhat timidly I gave the bin a couple of hits with my hand and the noises stopped for a moment, but then the sound of panting began again, a gurgling, raspy sound, seemingly emanating from a pair of froth-filled lungs. I was losing patience:

"Get out of there, whatever you are!"

You Erbo's chest and red neck emerged from the bin. I imagined at first that I was witnessing some kind of puppet show, but then the sun's rays streaming in through the skylight proved me wrong — there was You Erbo's long, pointed nose jutting out, stained a golden red by some liquid inside the bin. His chest underneath the white cotton undershirt was heaving uncontrollably, like waves tossing in a rain storm. He didn't utter a sound, but just stood there dumbly, like a frightened billy goat.

My playmates and I amused ourselves catching beetles and dragonflies, something we never tired of doing. Wild grasses, wild flowers, wild insects — at one time or another they all wound up in our hands, and it was like that from dawn to dusk. On nice clear evenings I went by myself into the clump of tall grass, where fireflies flitted to and fro, and where there was a constant murmur of insects in the tall grass, which cast evening shadows as it waved in the wind. Sometimes I stamped down the grass in one spot and lay down on top of it so that I could look up at the sky and the stars I loved so much. I had heard people talk about the ocean, and I envisioned it as about the same as my sky.

One evening at dinnertime I returned to the house from the clump of grass carrying some little boxes filled with insects, and as I passed by the grain storeroom I was startled to see You Erbo standing inside, his bluish lips and pale sunken eyes framed by the outline of the broken window.

"There isn't anyone in the compound, is there?" he asked in a throaty, sickly voice.

"Yes, there is; Ma's on the steps smoking."

"Okay. Go on!"

There wasn't a trace of a smile on his face; he seemed pale and his hair looked like the fur on the stray cat that ran back and forth on top of the wall.

Crouching on the bench at You Erbo's place at the dinner table was a little spotted dog with a curly tail and a brass bell around his neck, which really made him look adorable as he frolicked on the bench. Mother threw him a piece of meat. Then the crooked-necked cook picked a big bone out of the soup pot, which the spotted puppy chased frantically after jumping to the ground, the bell ringing out crazily. My little sister banged happily on her rice bowl with her chopsticks, the cook wiped his eyes with his apron, and Mother knocked over the soup bowl.

"Hurry . . . hurry and get a rag; hurry, it's spreading." Although she tried to cover her mouth with her hand, she still spit out rice grains as she spoke.

After the cook had cleared the dinner table he lit the kerosene lamp, and I sat on the threshold of the door looking out into the garden. The pale yellow light from the lamp silhouetted my head and shoulders, so that each time I raised my head to wipe the sweat off my brow, my shadow moved in concert with it. The evening breezes penetrating my cotton undershirt felt like cool, blue river water washing over me; the strains of a stringed instrument, the *huqin*, floated over from the grain shop on the street behind the house, and with the distant echo, sound came simultaneously from the east and the west. Flowers that were yellow during the day looked white, and those which were red now looked black.

The fiery red blossoms of the purslane plants too had become black, while the tiny flowers on the wild purslanes growing at the foot of the wall had completely disappeared from sight. Perhaps You Erbo had trampled on those little flowers, since he pressed himself up against the wall as he walked by. I followed him with my eyes, watching him as he went out the garden gate. He was totally unaware that I had come out and was following him. I was curious; what was he going to do with that thing he had stolen? He couldn't eat it, and it surely wouldn't be any fun to play with.

By the time I had reached the gate, he was already across the bridge, heading east on the wide, brightly lit road leading up to the tall hill. I imagined that the walls and gates standing along either side of the road in the moonlight were temples. Still watching the small round sack flung over You Erbo's back, I began to hear dogs barking in the distance in the direction he was heading.

The third time I saw him steal something, or maybe it was the fourth — anyway it was the last time — he was carrying our large bathtub on his shoulders as he cut across the garden, knocking down some dragon-head flowers as he went. Seemingly without a care, he walked with the loudly clanging tin bathtub over his head. It looked like a large piece of gleaming silver, and the sparkles which danced off it seemed scary to me, so I moved over beside the wall where I just stood like a simpleton.

I wondered if Mother would give him a beating if she caught him. I also felt some respect for him: would I have the nerve to steal something like that someday? But then the thought struck me: "Why steal something like that? Since it's so big, no matter where I put it, Mother'd be sure to find it." But You Erbo just kept walking along with it over his head, looking like the big snake in the storybook.

After that I never saw him steal anything again, but I did see some other things, even more risky ones and more often. Like, once in the tall grass when I had just caught a dragonfly by the tail, *kerplunk*, something like a big boulder came hurtling over the wooden wall, scaring the dragonfly off. I no longer dared to go over by the wooden wall to catch crickets in the evenings either, because I never knew when You Erbo might come crashing down. After the loss of the bathtub Mother started locking all three of the outside gates, so among all the kids who played around there I always caught the fewest crickets, and I began to resent You Erbo.

"You're always jumping over the wall, and I can't catch any more crickets!"

"Don't jump over the wall, that's easy to say, but who's going to open the gate for me?" His neck was sticking straight out.

"Yang An will open it, won't he?"

"Yang . . . An . . . hah! You're all part of the family and you can give him orders, but I. . . ."

"Don't you know how to yell? Call him, and then if he doesn't hear you, what's to stop you from beating on the gate?" I was swinging my arms as I talked.

"Hah! Beat on the door. . . ." His eyes were fixed on the ground in front of him.

"If he doesn't hear you beating on the door, then what's wrong with kicking it?"

"Kick a locked gate; what good would that do?"

"So there's no way but to climb over the wall, right? Then can't you do it gently, instead of scaring people out of their skins?"

"How can I do it gently?"

"Like when I jump down from the wall; no one hears a sound, because I crouch as I hit the ground, with my arms up in the air." I did a practice jump there on the level ground to show him.

"I could do that when I was young, but now that I'm old there's no way! My old bones are hard! I'm sixty years older than you; how can you compare the two of us?"

A wry smile appeared at the corner of his mouth. He held his tobacco pouch with his right hand and with his left stroked the ears of the big white dog standing next to him; the dog began to lick his hand. But I still didn't believe him; how could someone's bones be hard or soft? Weren't bones just bones? A pork bone was too hard for me to bite, and so was a mutton bone, so how could my bones be any different than his?

From then on, whenever I came across some bones I tried banging them against each other, and whenever I was with a playmate who was either older than I or a year younger, I invariably wanted to try an experiment. What sort of experiment? Well, we doubled up our fists and banged our knuckles together to see how much softer or harder they were. But I could never see much of a difference. If we hit a little harder it just hurt more. The first person I tested was Yaba, the caretaker's daughter. At first she wasn't willing, but I said to her:

"You're a year younger than I am, so let's give it a try; the smaller someone is, the softer the bones, so let's see if yours are softer than mine."

When we did, the knuckles on her fist turned red, so I thought: "Hers must be softer than mine." But then I looked and saw that mine were all red too.

One time You Erbo fell off the wall and bloodied his nose.

"Hah! I wasn't careful enough; one leg was dangling down, and the other was still hung up on the wall . . . hah! I tumbled head first."

He seemed to be mocking himself; since he didn't use his sleeve or anything else to wipe off the blood, to look at him you would have thought that it was someone else's nose that was bleeding. He stood up straight and walked off toward the side room, the blood continuing to stream profusely down the front of his clothes. His hand was bloodstained by now and dangling at his side, never moving up to stop the flow of blood. The cook, standing in the middle of the compound, cocked his head to one side and said:

"Master You, that's nice young blood you have there. I think even if you fell a couple more times it still wouldn't hurt you much."

"Hah! Little smart aleck . . . everybody starts out from youth and keeps on going! There's no need for you to be so sarcastic, your time will come one of these days." There was still a smile on his bloody mouth.

After a while You Erbo appeared in the doorway of the side room, bare-chested and bare-shouldered, with pieces of something stuffed up each nostril.

"Old Yang — Yang An, do you have a shirt I can wear? This one will be dry tomorrow, and then I'll take yours off. Since the sleeve on my other one is torn, I've ordered a lined jacket made, but I haven't found the time to go and get it." He was shaking out the garment he had just washed.

"What'd you say?" Yang An seemed almost to be shouting: "You haven't found the time to fetch the lined jacket you ordered? Our Master You sure is a busy man! His clothes are made, but he doesn't have the time to go get them. Master You truly *The Master*, and one of these days he'll be needing a valet."

I had climbed a ladder up to the roof over the side room in order to get a better view of a squabble that had erupted out on the street, but the wind up there was so strong I came down shivering. You Erbo was standing under the eaves still half naked, that wet garment of his hanging on a line and flapping in the wind. About the time the lamps were being lit I went back into the house to put on something warmer, and to my surprise there was You Erbo sitting alone at the dinner table drinking wine, and even more strangely, there was Yang An pouring out some soup for him.

"I can pour it myself! You go on and rest." You Erbo and Yang An were vying over the soup spoon. As I walked over to take a look I even saw a place with two slices of meat on it next to the wine decanter. You Erbo was wearing Yang An's short black jacket, his belt cinched up almost around his chest. He had never worn clothes that small before, and he didn't look to me at all like You Erbo, although just who he did look like I couldn't say. He was chewing on something, which made the plugs in his nose move and twitch.

As a rule only Father sat alone at the dinner table under the overhead light, eating his meal after returning home in the evening; for You Erbo this was unheard of, so I stood watching. Looking like a skinny doubled-over beetle, Yang An ran to the living room door:

"Come on and take a look!" He cocked his head: "Everyone says he doesn't eat mutton . . . doesn't eat mutton, eh; his stomach's so small, I'm afraid it's about to burst. He's already finished three big bowls of mutton soup . . . finished them . . . ha-ha-ha." He chuckled quietly, gestured with his hands, and then let the door curtain drop back into place.

On another occasion, when it wasn't even mutton soup but was made from beef stock, as soon as You Erbo picked up his spoon, Yang An said:

"Mutton soup. . . ."

He put down his spoon. Then as he picked up some fried eggplant with his chopsticks, Yang An said to him:

"Fried sheep's liver and eggplant."

He rinsed off his chopsticks, then went to the cupboard and took out a plate of pickled salted vegetables, but before he had gotten them back to the table, Yang An said:

"Sheep —" He didn't finish.

"What do you mean, sheep?" You Erbo stood looking at him.

"Sheep ... sheep ... um ... it's, uh, salted vegetables ... ahhh! I mean there's clean salted vegetables, and then there's unclean."

"What do you mean, unclean?"

"Well, I sliced the vegetables with my mutton knife."

"You can't do that to me, Yang An!" You Erbo walked away from the table and flung the plate on top of it. The table was so slippery the plate bounced around before bumping into another plate and coming to rest.

"You there, Yang An, don't go taking advantage of people. You're not a member of the Jiang family; just like me, you're an outsider here! Young people have to try to do good things ... shouldn't act like this. Some day you'll have your own posterity."

"Ha! Posterity? My line is gong to die with me. But your not eating sheep's intestines is as phony as the fish smell of pastry fish frying at the dough shop. You don't eat sheep's intestines but then you go ahead and eat mutton; stop putting on that act." Yang An was so angry his neck stiffened a little.

"You hare-brained queer! God damn it, what are you getting so huffy about?" You Erbo stood up and walked toward him.

"Master You, don't get yourself so worked up, you'll make yourself sterile that way. Listen to me, we're both a couple of poor working stiffs; it was just a joke, all in fun." The cook snickered: "There wasn't any sheep's intestine in it; I was just having some fun; don't take it all so seriously."

You Erbo stood there like a statue. "I don't get angry at other things, and I'm not afraid of a little joke, but here I draw the line — this is more than a joke. The year before last I ate some without knowing it; then when I found out, I was ill for over half a month. A boil had developed here on my neck before I got better. Eating a piece of mutton didn't hurt me, but thinking about it made me uneasy, as if I had gone against my own conscience. If I hadn't done something against my conscience — But I did, and I couldn't bear my feelings of regret. And that's why I don't eat mutton." He took a drink of cold water, then lit his pipe.

One after the other the rest of us began leaving the table.

From then on You Erbo's nose often had plugs of some sort stuck up it. Later he began complaining of a sore back, then of sore legs. Walking across the compound, he was no longer as erect as before — sometimes there was a pronounced lean to his body, and sometimes he was seen walking with his hand holding onto his belt. When the big white dog trailed along behind him, jumping back and forth, he tried to avoid it:

"Go on, go on!" He pulled his hand up inside his sleeve, which he flapped in the air behind him.

But then he started cursing even smaller things; like, when he stubbed his toe on a piece of brick he sat on the ground and held the piece of brick down tightly with his hand, as if he suspected it had deliberately moved over in front of his foot. Or if there were birds flying overhead and droppings landed on his sleeve, he would shake them off, turn his head toward the sky, and tell the birds, who by then had flown off already:

"You dirty... hah! You sure know how to aim, bang onto my sleeve. What are you, blind? If you have to drop something, drop it on someone who's wearing silk or satin! Drop it on me and you just waste... you bunch of crippled beggars..."

He would wipe his sleeve clean, take another look at the sky, and continue on his way.

There were no longer any crickets to be found at the foot of the wooden wall, though You Erbo evidently had stopped climbing over it. When the cook went out in the morning to fetch water, You Erbo went out the gate behind the water bucket, then headed toward the well and sat down on the old millstone beside it. Almost every day, when I took the key out to open the gate and let my playmates in, he called out from there on the millstone:

"Huazi, wait for me." He looked like a duck waddling along. "I'm really having my problems; I could see... I could see the kids coming this way, but I couldn't catch up with them."

As soon as he came in the gate he sat down on a wooden wine cask off to the side. One foot had a sock on it, but the toes of the other were wrapped with a piece of hemp. He loosened the hemp wrapping, and underneath the piece of cloth covering his swollen toes (which looked like little eggplants), a piece of skin was rotting away. Then he wrapped the foot up again with the cloth.

"My luck this year has been all bad... one problem after another." He reached up and removed a piece of hemp he'd been holding in his mouth.

The Family Outsider

After that whenever I let my playmates in, it wasn't You Erbo who called out to me, but me who called out to him, because if I closed the gate and then he walked up to it from outside, I was the one who had to go back and open it for him. Not only did he sit there on the millstone, but gradually he even took to sleeping there. He slept as if he were in a coma. Once a brightly colored duck stretched its neck out and pecked him on the soles of his feet, but he didn't wake up, and his feet stayed stretched out just where they were. With the sun's rays dancing off the millstone, it looked like he was sleeping on a large round mirror.

One day some of the kids and I were throwing stones and dirt at each other, running out of the gate and over to the well where there was plenty of ammunition. I stuffed my pockets full of stones and crouched behind the millstone, doing battle with the rest of the kids. *Pow! Pow!* The stones fell onto the millstone, raising a cloud of dust. You Erbo, his eyes still closed, suddenly grabbed his tobacco pouch:

"You little bastards, what's going on? How dare you come ... how dare you climb up ..."

He struck out to his left and right, and after we had all gathered around him, he finally sat up.

"Damn it, I was having a dream ... dogs all over that road. And even the mongrel pups were coming at me. I finally drove them all off with the bowl of my pipe." He rubbed his knuckles as a smile spread across his face: "I'll be damned, it sure was life-like; I dreamt about getting bitten by a pack of dogs, and now that I'm awake I can still feel the pain."

It was obvious that our stones were responsible, but he said it was the "mongrel pups," and the whole affair both alarmed and delighted us. When we left him we scattered like a flock of chickens, shouting and spreading our "wings."

He yawned, making sounds like a donkey braying; we turned back to see him facing the sun, his open mouth making swallowing motions.

One drizzly morning as You Erbo was sitting out on the millstone, Yang An carried his bucket out several times to fetch water, and the last time he locked the gate behind him.

"These past few days Master You has changed a lot," he said. "The way he looks now, I'm afraid we'll be carrying him into the temple before many more days have passed."

I looked out to the west through the crack in the gate, but I couldn't see You Erbo clearly — he just looked like a haystack soaking up the rain.

"You Erbo, it's time to eat!" I tried calling out to him, but the only answer I got was an echo from my own voice: "You Erbo, it's time to eat!" Then I put my mouth right up against the crack in the gate, but again the only answer I got was my own echo. A rainy day always seemed more like nighttime to me, like an empty bottle that whistled with every puff of wind.

"Don't worry about that one," Mother said as she opened the window. "He's just looking for trouble. These last few days your father has been thinking of a way to fix him."

I knew what that "fix him" meant: when you hit a child it's called a "beating," but when you hit an adult it's called "fixing him." Once I had seen our caretaker "fix" You Erbo over a game of cards, but I had never seen Father do it.

Mother said to Yang An: "These last few years my husband has just ignored him and has never once raised a hand against him, but the man's insufferable arrogance is getting worse and worse. The no-good loafer won't be happy until someone fixes him."

The more Mother used the words "fix him," the more frightened I grew; where would he "fix him"? In the middle of the compound? That isn't where the caretaker did it — that time it happened on the *kang* in the side room. Maybe that's where it would happen this time too! Would he use the fireplace poker? That's what the caretaker had used. Then I recalled that once little Yaba had had her finger stepped on by the caretaker and nearly got it broken; it still wasn't very straight.

As he knocked on the gate You Erbo called out:

"You big white ... big white, you don't have an ounce of decency. One of these days you'll ..." When the dog jumped down off the wall, You Erbo said: "Go on, get out ..."

"Open the gate! Isn't there anyone inside?"

Just as I was about to run over there, Mother put her hand on my head and stopped me: "Don't be in such a hurry! Let him stand there awhile; he's not the one who's feeding you."

The noise from the gate grew louder, and he seemed to have started kicking.

"Isn't anyone there?" He was almost shouting.

"There's someone here all right, but no one to wait on you, you useless old fool!"

I don't know whether or not You Erbo could hear what Mother was saying, but a furious storm of noise erupted at the gate: "Are you all dead in there? Is everyone inside dead or something?"

"Don't you start acting like a madman. Who are you cursing at? Have we treated you badly or something?" Mother was shouting from the kitchen. "Whose food have you been eating half your life? You give it some thought when you can't sleep; if you had any self-respect you wouldn't be here eating our rice. What right has a beggar to complain that the food is spoiled?"

There was no answer. A rumbling noise came from beyond the wall, and when we saw him he was already standing on this side.

"I — I want to say — Sister-in-Law, I was talking about Yang An. I wasn't talking about anyone in the family; it's true I'm useless, but you needn't grudge a bowl of rice." Even though a fight was about to break out, or so I thought, there was still a smile on his face as he said: "If my brother were here I could settle this with him."

"Your brother? Do you think he would stoop to settling the matter with you?!" Mother stepped back and pushed me away.

"Wouldn't stoop to settle the matter with his elder brother, hah! One day we'll just see about that. One day when my brother isn't in school, then we'll have this out." He stood there huffing, his brimless hat that looked like an earthenware bowl cutting across his forehead. As he walked across the compound each footstep left a deep impression in the mud.

"That wretched devil just won't die! Even with his foot rotting off, he still manages to jump over the wall!" It seemed that Mother wanted him to hear this.

"Ah, Sister-in-Law, you're talking about your elder brother, humph, humph! How can you talk to me like that? Me die . . . you shouldn't curse me like that; we're all raised by our parents and eat the same food as we grow up." He jerked open the door of the side room as if it were made of stone, but he didn't go inside. "I've lived here with you for more than thirty years, and what have I ever done to you? You check your conscience; I've never trampled down a single blade of your grass... *ai!* Sister-in-Law, this year — I can't express it. No way at all. How can you tell what's in a person's heart?"

I slid down and hopped across the compound to the side room, my hands full of persimmons, where I found You Erbo in front of a warm fire. He was sitting there as straight and motionless as the empty urn just inside the door.

"Scram, you little witch! What do you want? Your whole family are rats," he said. I just stood in the doorway, without even going inside, and that's the sort of abuse he greeted me with. No wonder Yang An said that You Erbo had changed, I thought to myself. Even when he was using abusive language he uttered strange expressions I didn't really understand; what did "rats" have to do with me? Why bring them up? I was still in the doorway when he said:

"Bastard kid... hare-brained queer... wretch... cur... not a human being... haven't got what it takes to be a person." He rambled on, one curse after another, and I don't remember what all he said.

Just like he usually did, I took off my shoes and put them on the floor, soles together, then sat on them.

"You're quite a kid; whatever someone else does, you do the same thing. You see a gourd and right away you paint a calabash. A good pair of new shoes, and you sit right on top of them." He looked at me with those eyes of his like the small pits on carelessly fired urns.

"What about you then?" I put my hand out near the fire.

"I sit on — just take a look at my shoes; it doesn't make any difference if I sit on them or not, because they're beyond repair! I've already worn these for two years." He took his shoes out from under him, put them up near the fire, and looked at them for a long time. Suddenly he got angry: "You folks, you live in a paradise. When I was your age I didn't have any shoes — where would I have gotten them? Out herding pigs with nothing but a little whip — out in the morning with the rising sun, back with the setting sun, only a couple of rice balls to take along for lunch. But look at the rest of you — *mantou* and grain flowing all over the compound! If I went out and swept the compound I could pick up quite a few. When I was young I never touched even a crumb of *mantou*! Now even the dog turns up his nose at them."

If no one cut off this monologue of his, he could keep it up forever: he talked about the years when he was growing up, then about the clay pot on the stove, and from the clay pot he returned to his youth and the rice balls he had had to eat. I knew the whole routine, and I was sick of hearing it, so I went up to the stove and started roasting my persimmons to see how they would turn out.

"Go on, get out of here; I never saw a brat like you. A person can't even warm himself at a fire; you'll wind up putting it out. Go on, go roast them somewhere else!" he shouted as he watched the fire.

I put on my shoes and bolted out the door; since it remained open, his abuse continued to ring out loudly:

"You little witch, what the hell do you think you're

doing? Your whole family is nothing but a bunch of rats!"

Just like the eggplants in the rear garden, You Erbo was grayish and pale, but the older the eggplants got, the quieter and calmer their appearance, as if they were completely resigned to their fate. You Erbo, on the other hand, railed from one end of the compound to the other, hurling abuses at everything from the yard broom to the water barrel, and eventually even his own straw hat: "Bastard... what kind of trash are you? You just get away from me... no damn human feelings! You don't make it any cooler in the summer and don't add any warmth in the winter."

Eventually he put his hat on anyway and followed Yang An's water bucket out the gate to the well, but instead of sitting down on the millstone, he followed the water bucket right back.

"Bastard... you're not even a beast with that black heart of yours," he yelled to the pig along the base of the wall, then turned around and spotted a flock of ducks: "One of these days I'm going to kill you all... day in and day out, *quack, quack, quack;* God damn it, if you were human beings you'd be a lazy bunch of bums. Kill you all... don't figure yourselves lucky, just eat, eat,... get nice and plump..."

The sunflower seeds in the rear garden were all ripe; the heavy heads of the flowers seemed about to make their bodies snap in two. Some of the corn stalks stood there with nothing but green leaves on them, while on others a few ears of corn hung here and there. As always, the cucumbers were spread out over the trellis, their brownish skins all spotted and cracked. Some were girded with red bands, having been selected by Mother for seeds to be used next year. The same was true for the sunflowers; red strips of cloth were hanging from many of their necks. Only the aging, pale gray eggplants were left undisturbed on branches; since only black seeds were inside, the children wouldn't eat them, and so the cook didn't bother with them. But the red persimmons quickly assumed their scarlet coloring, one after another, cluster after cluster, resembling nothing so much as the sound of clothes being beaten with mallets, coming at you endlessly from all directions.

One crisp, early morning, to the sound of clothes being beaten, You Erbo collapsed in the compound. All of us children gathered round him, as did many of the neighbors, but when he began to pick himself up, the neighbors backed away and cleared a path for him. He ran back, then fell to the ground again; Father didn't seem to have done much at all — he merely gave You Erbo a knock on the head. This scene repeated itself several times, with You Erbo looking something like a coiling-worm flailing around on the ground. Father was as efficient as a machine. He still had his reading glasses on, standing with his legs apart, and each time You Erbo came over to him, I saw the corner of the sleeve of his white satin gown move gracefully:

"You Erbo, you no-account bastard, all day long all you do is shout abuses. You have enough to eat and drink. What the hell else do you want, you son-of-a-bitch?"

You Erbo didn't make a sound in reply. After falling to the ground once more, he struggled back to his feet, walked up to where Father was, and was promptly knocked to the ground once again. By the time he had fallen to the ground yet another time, the neighbors had stopped gathering round him. All this time Mother was standing on the steps; Yang An watched from beside the pile of firewood, holding a bamboo broom in front of him; and the old granny from next door was just on the other side of the gate, the blue flowers in her hair tossing in the wind. Then there was the caretaker, and little Yaba, plus some people I didn't recognize, all standing over near the wall. Eventually You Erbo's head was pillowed in his own blood, and he got up no more; the hempen wrapping from around his toes was lying beside him, and there was nothing left of the little round gourd from his tobacco pouch but a clutter of shreds to his left. A rooster crowed, but then scrambled off into the distance; only some ducks came over to peck at the blood on the ground. I could see one with a green head and another with a spotted neck.

By the time winter arrived the elm tree had shed all its leaves; as it stood there alone, every gust of wind from the west struck it with full force. So every night as I listened to the whistling of the steam kettle on the stove I looked out the back window at that big tree — all white, it seemed covered with a layer of goose feathers, even the smallest branch looking thicker than usual. In the daytime rays of the sun the elm took on a sparkle, like the glints of light dancing on the roofs or the ground.

We first busied ourselves with making snowmen until we tired of that, then switched to having the dog pull us on a sled. Every single day there was a rope fastened around the big white dog's neck. We used a sled that Yang An made for us, but instead of pulling us along the roads, the dog always ran toward his doghouse or the kitchen. After we hit him often enough, he began to get used to it, but still he often just ran around in a circle, sooner or later dumping us all in the snow. And every time he did this we simply didn't feed him for a whole day, and we even put a muzzle over his mouth. But he never learned to accept this punishment, running around and making an awful racket, and pawing at the snow-covered ground, so we always wound up tying him to the hitching post.

Once, for some unexplained reason, You Erbo untied the dog with violently shaking hands. Then he led him over to the side room, as if he were leading a horse. After a while he came out, followed by the dog, on whose back was piled a number of things: a straw hat, a brass water jug, an oil cup for a lamp, a square pillow, a fan made of rushes, a round basket — he looked like a little cart used on moving day. You Erbo carried his bedding under his arm.

"Erbo, are you going home?"

He kept mumbling, "Let's go, let's go," and I thought "let's go" must mean "go home."

"I — um —" The snow on the ground was spotted with all the pieces of cotton that were falling out of his bedding, a bunch of black ash-like flecks bouncing around on top of the snow. Before he had reached the gate the dog stopped abruptly, and even though You Erbo hit him, he seemed unable to get him to move anymore:

"So you're not going to go! You ... big white ..."

I fetched the key and opened the gate for him. At the edge of the well all the stuff on the dog's back flipped over; the little round basket, the brass water jug, and all the other things ended up on top of the millstone.

"You Erbo, are you going home?" If he wasn't planning on going home, then why take all this stuff with him?

"Um, I . . ." By then the dog had run a long ways off. "This isn't my home, but I don't have a home anywhere else either. Come on," he called out to the dog, "you don't have to carry anything; just come here." He spread open his arms as if he was going to embrace the dog. "I wanted to wait until spring came, but there's no way." When he picked up the brass water jug and all the rest of the stuff, I thought for sure he was leaving. I looked at the main gate way off in the middle of all that snow. But he turned around and headed back toward the wooden gate, walking like someone carrying a water barrel on his shoulders, wobbling from side to side.

"Erbo, did you forget something?"

The only answer I got was the *clang-clang* of the brass rings on the water jug. Was he going after the dog? I was growing more and more interested in the whole episode, so I left my playmates and followed along behind him. When he reached the doorway of the side room he walked in, without, it seemed, even noticing the muzzled dog.

What was it he had forgotten? But rather than fetch anything, he just sat down on the edge of the *kang*, that whole pile of junk still resting on his back or hanging down in front of his chest. As he began to talk, I instinctively drew closer.

"Huazi, close the door and come here!" He pushed all the stuff off his body. "Come here and take a look!"

What was I supposed to be looking at?

He lifted up the grass sleeping mat and grabbed a handful of something.

"Just look at this." He threw some kernels of grain to the ground: "It's clear as can be that this was meant to drive me away. Though nobody cares about my aching back and legs, at least I could be thankful for this warm bed! Now they say they're out of rice, and since this grain is still wet, they put it here under my mat to dry out for a few days. It's been more than ten days already... more than an inch thick... but the heat can still reach the top if there's a fire going. *Ai* I'd better wait until spring comes. These clothes are no good for cold weather."

He picked up the broom and swept the frost and snow off the windowsill, then swept the wall.

"See all this; if it were sugar I could eat without spending any money!"

Finally, after he lit a fire and put a pile of firewood and dry grass beside the opening beneath the kang stove, frost and ice began dripping off his beard as it melted; tears were running down my face, as both of us were engulfed in the smoke belching out. He told me he had been bitten by a wolf when he was seven, and at eight had lost a toe when he was kicked by a donkey.

"Tell me the truth, have you ever seen a tiger in the mountains?" I asked.

"No, that I've never seen," he said.

"How about an elephant?"

He didn't answer my question, but said that he had herded draft oxen for a few years and pigs for several more.

"I lost my mother when I was only three months old ... my father when I was six months old ... lived with my uncle for the first seven years, until just about your age now."

"What about when you were just about my age?" My interest began to wane as he moved away from the subject of wolves and tigers.

"When I was about your age I started herding pigs for people."

"You were just about my age when the wolf bit you, weren't you? After that did you ever dare to go back up the mountain again?"

"Dare? ... hah! In your own home you're a pampered child, but when you live in other people's homes, you have to be an adult. No, I didn't dare. Sure I was afraid. I cried over it, and suffered a few good beatings too."

"Were you only bitten once by a wolf?"

He dropped the subject of wolves altogether and began talking about other things: how during such-and-such a year he had worked for someone feeding their horses; how my grandfather had brought him back home; then there was something about the cherry blossoms during the month of May. Then: "The last few years I've been giving some thought to taking a wife."

I could tell that he was starting in on his regular routine so I bolted out of the room and stood in the middle of the compound. I couldn't see a thing out of my smoke-filled red eyes, from which tears were still streaming, but You Erbo just lay down beside the pile of firewood and began to weep softly.

I walked up toward the main house, the sun at my back and the ground sparkling around me, surrounding me with its glitter; it was there in front beckoning me, and behind me driving me forward. I stood on the steps and looked around at all those pure white, sparkling rooftops and the glittering tree branches. It looked as if dozens of trees carved out of white coral were standing amid the cluster of buildings.

The louder You Erbo's weeping grew, the lovelier all my surroundings seemed to me. How close they all were: the snow was under my feet, and all those rooftops and tree branches were my neighbors! And though the sun was rather far away, still it came to shine down on my head.

In the spring I entered one of the neighborhood elementary schools.

I didn't see You Erbo any more after that.

Flight from Danger

HOW'S a person expected to get on that train? With baggage it's impossible; even for people, the only way to get aboard is for someone down below to boost them up.

Before the War of Resistance He Nansheng was an elementary school teacher. After fleeing from Nanjing he came to Shaanxi, where he met a friend who was a middle-school principal. So He Nansheng became a middle-school teacher. But before going into this, we'll take a look at his appearance. You could feel sad for him just by looking at his face. His two sparkling eyes were forever surveying things carefully, although the things that other people looked at he consciously avoided, and the things others avoided were the very things that attracted his stealthy glances. Before he started to speak, his mouth spread open on all four sides, gradually giving it the appearance of a matchbox; anyone noticing this assumed he might have bitten into something bitter. His face had another peculiar feature: regardless of whether he was laughing, talking or frowning, the two square patches of muscle that puffed out like a couple of pieces of beancurd just under his eye socket never moved the slightest bit. Not even his best friend or, for that matter, his wife, had ever seen those two brick-like patches of muscle so much as twitch.

"What's going on here . . . these people! I tell you, if there's any hope at all for the Chinese, I'll be God-damned if I "

He Nansheng had always been anti-Chinese; it was almost as though he were not Chinese himself. Although before the war of resistance he had been almost violently anti-Chinese, after the outbreak of war he softened his attitude a little. Then there was his old defect, which came to the surface every once in a while.

Just what was that defect of his? Well, whenever he was heading toward a difficult situation, even if it failed to materialize, the minute he began to contemplate something unpleasant happening to him in the future he grew dissatisfied with the whole world. Situations like the following: his socks might nearly be chewed on by mice after he had taken them off at night; or, on his way down from the lectern he might step on a piece of chalk and nearly fall down as the chalk rolled under his foot. In a word, if the danger failed to materialize and nothing at all came of the matter, for him the thought of what might have happened disturbed him unbelievably. So besides his penchant for saying what he thought about the Chinese, there was another sentence he habitually uttered, and that was:

"What'll I do when the time comes?"

He turned around and took another look at the train that was so jammed with people it looked more like a cage filled with ducks.

"What'll I do when the time comes?" What he meant by this was what would he do when the time came to flee.

He Nansheng and his wife were seeing a colleague off. Dissatisfaction was upon him before he had even left the platform, for the first thing he saw after taking his eyes off the train was his wife. To him she looked as big and fat as a clumsy pig, and that would add considerably to the problems of being refugees.

"There, you see; what'll I do when the time comes?" "If she were any fatter," he mused, "even an entire railroad car wouldn't be big enough to hold her!" But he refrained from saying this aloud.

Then his thoughts turned to the two children, the willow suitcase, the pigskin suitcase, the net-covered basket and the three quilts that all had to be taken. He had left enough room in the netcovered basket to fit two iron cooking pots, for they'd surely have to cook wherever they went. As refugees wouldn't they have to eat no matter where they fled to? Actually, the word "refugee" is superfluous here; as I see it, those who daily mouth the words "War of Resistance" are the first to become refugees when the time to flee approaches, and on top of that, they take their wives, kids and a great pile of pots, pans, bowls and basins.

On the way back he walked ahead of his wife, for the simple reason that whenever he was disturbed he didn't feel like looking at anything. He walked with his neck thrust forward, his shoulders slumped and his arms looking as though they were made of straw. Not even the tips of his fingers moved as he walked. With the exception of his legs, which moved one in front of the other, he looked exactly like one of those paper funerary figures displayed in shops that sold such artwork.

Over the past few days He Nansheng had been quite anxious about his family, owing mainly to the unshakeable image of that train in which the people were so tightly packed they were nearly immobilized; it was the one he had seen when he sent his colleague off. But then, even without any thoughts of being a refugee or any War of Resistance, even during the most usual, uneventful times, he never failed to be in a state of terror. Came the War of Resistance, and he concluded that it was absolutely hopeless to even contemplate any personal happiness. So he immediately began to prepare himself for misfortune. How you ask, is that possible? Let me counsel the reader not to be surprised, for He Nansheng is about to illustrate this for us: On March 15, 1938, the first thing he saw as he got out of bed was the calendar he had placed in readiness on the wall.

"Ah, of course, today's the day — it's the 15th . . ." He hadn't slept well all night, for his thoughts had kept him awake the entire time — one after another thought of every matter imaginable, major or minor, until he heard the sounds of artillery at Laodong Pass.

An artillery battle between us and the enemy occupying Fenglingdu across the river had been raging for several days; artillery fire ceased at night, only to start up again at the crack of dawn. Actually, it was nothing to be afraid of, and He Nansheng was undisturbed. For even though the school where he was teaching was less than a hundred *li* from Laodong Pass, close enough that he should have been frightened, all of his belongings were packed and ready and he was about to leave — so who cared, artillery battle or no artillery battle!

The second thing he saw was a pair of socks his wife had placed alongside the pillow for him.

"What're these for? We're about to take flight . . . we're not going to assume a new official appointment, you know . . . do you have any idea how much a pair of socks costs these days . . ." He barked an order: "Hurry and bring me a pair of old socks! And put this new pair away."

He stuck his foot into a slipper without noticing how worn the old sock was; when his wife saw his foot sticking out through the heel she began to snicker.

"What're you laughing at? Laughing, hah! What's so funny about that . . . and why aren't you dressing the children? It's getting late . . . getting on one of those trains is harder than climbing to Heaven. Didn't you see how it was the other day? What's so funny about a sock with a hole in it? You've never seen soldiers on the front lines, that's for sure — they're all barefoot!" To hear him you'd think he had witnessed such a sight himself, but in fact he hadn't.

He didn't go to his eleven o'clock or his one o'clock history classes, for he planned to be at the train station by two.

As he ate lunch he alternately looked at the clock and mopped his brow — he always broke out into a sweat when he was nervous. When the students asked what time the train was to leave, he told them:

"There's one at six o'clock and another at eight. I'll be taking the six o'clock train. Since everything is so unpredictable these days, the earlier the better. Besides, I'm taking them with me . . ." The "them" were his children, his wife and their baggage.

Since he was advisor to the student-organized War of Resistance National Salvation Club, he had to say a few words to the students before he left. Rather than give a prepared talk, he simply said that in four or five days he would be back — actually, once he left, he was gone for good — and ended by declaring that the final victory belonged to our side. In addition, he told them that his fate was tied up with that of Shaanxi — they would survive or perish together — and that he would never flee.

At 5:20 He Nansheng's entire household was all together at the train station: There was his wife, the children — one boy and one girl — a willow suitcase, a pigskin suitcase, a net-covered basket and three rolls of bedding. Why so many rolls of bedding? Because one was wrapped around his umbrella, waste-paper basket and some old newspapers, making a bundle; another was wrapped around a cotton uniform given to him by the War of Resistance National Salvation Club, and a pair of worn cotton shoes, making a second bundle; the third roll constituted a bundle with a great number of items: light bulbs, a chalk box, a lamb's-hair brush, a broom for the beds, two or three tattered rags, a large handful of wax candles, an abacus, about twenty feet of thin wire, a roll of white thread, plus the lid of a soapdish — the rest was old newspapers.

Just in old newspapers alone he was taking more than fifty catties; his reasoning: Won't we have to cook once we get where we're going? Won't we have to eat? And what's better for starting a fire than old newspaper? When living the life of a refugee, you have to economize wherever you can; if you manage to keep from starving, you're doing well.

Next to these three bundles, the net-covered basket had the greatest wealth of objects: steel cooking pots, black earthenware jars, empty cracker tins, curved wooden coat hangers, some clothesline, a chipped spittoon made in Shaanxi, a small piece of oilcloth that they put on the two-year-old girl's bed at night in case she wet her pants, plus two broken wash basins, one for washing faces and one for washing feet. Then there was a greasy chopstick holder, a kitchen knife, a pile of chopsticks, thirty or more ricebowls and three cutting boards. The cutting boards and ricebowls had been given to him by a friend who had already left. He reasoned that for a refugee, the more you fled, the fewer your possessions; it never worked out that the more you fled, the more plentiful your possessions. So it was advisable, whenever possible, to start off with a little more — that was undeniable — because if you lost one you still had the other, and even if you just threw everything away, you could at least spend a few extra days doing it! Then there were several pairs of tattered trousers at the bottom of the net-covered basket, and these too he had plans for.

When his wife was packing the net-covered basket she had asked him:

"What do you want these tattered trousers for?"

"Just listen to you," he said. "You have to make plans for every contingency. If we ever find ourselves in a refugee camp, won't these all come in handy?"

And so under his leadership his family finally arrived in a body at 5:20, coming perilously close to missing the train, which was to leave at six o'clock.

Perspiring freely, He Nansheng figured that this time everything had been taken care of satisfactorily, and he was about eighty percent happy; he couldn't think of a single thing he had forgotten to bring along, since by now he had already made three trips back and forth. The first time was for a flower vase, the second to take down a lampshade, and the third time for a half pack of Daopai cigarettes he had left beside the stove.

Since the train station was close to his home, he turned back to look at that little house of his which had been white until only yesterday; it had just been painted gray out of a fear of the airplanes. He lit a cigarette and puffed on it as he strolled around the platform. After all, they only had to wait until the train arrived, just that short time.

"What'll I do when the time comes?" According to precedent, this is what he should have been saying, with who-knows-how-many pieces of luggage and bundles up on the platform, and all those wounded and blooded soldiers and the crowd of clamoring refugees congregated there. They were all waiting to get onto the six o'clock train for Xian. But He Nansheng looked at things differently than others, and no matter what the situation that began to materialize, his initial reaction was one of timidity, or, in a word, despair. But then when the situation was truly at hand or was drawing nearer and nearer or was within sight, then you'd see him calm down considerably.

The train was due to arrive any minute — the clock on the platform said 5:41.

He surveyed his belongings one more time; large and small together, there were six pieces, plus one vacuum bottle.

"I'm sure we haven't forgotten a single thing! Now think hard, is there anything else?" he asked his wife.

His daughter, who had stumbled and fallen, was crying, so his wife was wiping her runny nose with her hand:

"Oh! I forgot my little handkerchief. I washed it this morning and hung it on the line in the yard. I kept thinking, now don't forget to take it, but that's exactly what I did. I had a feeling there was something else . . . I just knew there was something, but I couldn't think of what it was."

He Nansheng had long since left his wife standing there and was running back home.

"We couldn't just leave it there! Do you know how much a handkerchief like this costs these days?" He was using it to wipe the perspiration from his face. "Haven't I told you what refugee life is all about? If we run short of things, then we have to economize, since there's no way of replenishing our supply."

He let out a gasp as he rubbed his hand across his pocket, for the new pair of socks that he had been loath to put on in the morning had disappeared.

"Now where could they have been lost? God-damn it . . . the train'll be here any minute . . . thirty or forty cents, just thrown out the window!"

The train was behind schedule and had not arrived by 6:05, so he took advantage of the delay to run home one more time. He found the socks after all, and with them laid across his palm, he was examining the pattern when he heard his wife say:

"Your glasses! . . ."

Sure enough, when he touched his eyes there were no glasses there. He wasn't really near-sighted, but since he thought they improved his appearance, he wore them anyway.

Just as he was thinking of going back to look for his glasses, the train arrived.

He picked up his suitcases and ran toward the train. But with all his squeezing and pushing, he didn't manage to get on. He could see that others were faster on their feet than he, or maybe their baggage was lighter.

He'd been the first one up to the door of the car. Then why hadn't he climbed up instead of letting others get ahead of him? Some ten minutes later he and his baggage were still standing outside the railroad car.

"The Chinese, the God-damn . . . that's what the Chinese are like!" This outburst was sparked by his hat having gotten knocked off in the confusion.

The train had departed and was heading off in the distance, while He Nansheg and his entire family were still standing there on the platform.

"God-damn it, those Chinese are fleeing for their lives, but they'll kill themselves in the process! Resistance? Better they should call it desertion!" As soon as he uttered the word "desertion" he took a quick look around to see if any of his students were on the platform. He was in luck on that score, so he shook out his now-ripped long gown and muttered: "How can it have come to this? You haven't even seen a glimpse of the enemy and you're already scared out of your skins. Stampeding yourselves to death! You'd think there was a cannon dumping shells on your tails."

When the eight o'clock train for Xian rolled in, He Nansheng led his family in another assault on one of the railroad cars, his wife yelling, his children crying and the suitcases and net-covered basket creaking and scraping in the crush of people. He Nansheng had a vague feeling that he had fallen down, and when he picked himself up blood was flowing freely from his nose, staining the front of his long gown. His wife reported to him that their pigskin suitcase had travelled over the heads of the people and been conveyed right into the railroad car.

"What was in it?" In his flustered state he couldn't

even remember what had been packed into that particular suitcase.

"You mean you don't know? Weren't all your clothes in there? Your suits. . ."

This news hit him like a bombshell. He asked his wife to point out the car it was in, then ran after it. The train started up, slowly at first, and he kept up with it as he ran alongside, shouting, until gradually he found himself being outdistanced. He stopped and went back.

His whole family was once again left standing on the platform along with all the other people who had failed to make it onto the train. Only their pigskin suitcase had managed to board the train and was on its way.

"We didn't make it, we *didn't* make it. Who told you to take all this worn-out junk?" his wife grumbled. "As far as I'm concerned . . ."

"Don't take it, don't take it! Don't take a damned thing . . . what'll we do when the time comes!"

"Then you take it! We'll just see just what you manage to take!"

The pigskin suitcase had left its master and set out on its own; the stuffed net-covered basket was resting up against a railway tie, its belly split open; and the little iron pot was flattened pitifully, so dented that only its owner could have recognized it for what it was. The earthenware jars were smashed to smithereens. Of the three rolls of bedding, only one was complete, and it was on this roll that their two children were now sitting. One of the other rolls had disappeared, while the remaining one was ripped open, the old newspapers it had once contained now flying all around the platform.

The willow suitcase, too, had disappeared, but he couldn't recall if someone had taken it from him or if he put it aboard the train himself.

He Nansheng and his family made it onto the third train for Xian. The first thing they did upon their arrival was go to a friend's house.

"Ah, so you've made it! Is everything all right? The train wasn't too crowded, was it?"

"No, no, it's just that we lost a few things... but that's all right, it doesn't matter, since we're all fine." Those two patches under his eye that never moved were as unflinching as ever.

"What'll I do when . . ." He was about to say, "What'll I do when the time comes." but didn't — he decided to just drop it. Before victory in the War of Resistance, what could a person have that he could confidently say belonged to him? But after the victory, then won't we have everything we want?

He Nansheng calmly picked up the vacuum bottle he had carried along with him and put it on the table.

Vague Expectations

> 360 days in a year
> Each of them a day of agonies
> A life worse than the birds in the mountains
> A life worse than the cicadas in the fields....

On this day, after learning that Jin Lizhi was being sent to the front lines, Li Ma began singing this tune. Jin Lizhi was one of Laoye's* bodyguards. No one was aware of what was going on, although one of the other bodyguards might have known that something was up; then, that may have only been her imagination.

"Li Ma, Li Ma . . ."

Taitai's** shouts came to her from the shade of the trees, to which Li Ma quickly responded with two or three answering calls. By nature impetuous and spirited, this had always been her way, to this very day. But as she turned to go, she barely avoided tripping over the little bamboo stool beside her. She realized she was perspiring, her ears felt hot and she saw spots before her eyes.

"What lousy luck!" she thought. Noticing the other bodyguard alongside her, she checked herself from saying it aloud.

---

* Master.
** Mistress.

She returned from Taitai's side, carrying two tea glasses, and just as she was about to put them into the sink to wash them, the bodyguard named Wang cocked his head to one side and said:

"Be careful, Li Ma. What's there to get flustered about? Or, you'll break the glasses."

"What's there to get flustered about, you ask . . ." She stopped short of saying what was on her mind, then, in mock anger, purposely clinked the two glasses.

The glow from Taitai and Laoye's cigarettes in the middle of the grassy courtyard suddenly flared up like red flowers. Then the glow receded and flattened out like fallen petals from withered flowers. Lightning bugs darted back and forth among the leaves in the trees, looking like they were suspended in the sky and helplessly blown about by the wind.

"There surely won't be any alarm tonight . . ." Taitai tilted her chair backwards and glanced up at the sky. She wasn't altogether convinced that the sky was completely overcast, and was searching the heavens to try to find a star somewhere.

"Taitai, hasn't it been several nights since we heard an alarm?" Li Ma seemed to have been swallowed up in the darkness of the night.

"No, it'll come in the next few days. As soon as the fighting crosses the Yangtze River, the air raids over Wuhan will increase . . ."

"How far will the war carry, Taitai? Will it go as far as Hubei?"

"I'm sure it will. Aren't you aware that Jin Lizhi is going up to the front lines?"

"To Daye. Taitai, just where is this Daye? How far from here?"

"Not too far. It's an iron-producing area. Jin Lizhi and the entire special service company is going there."

"Does a special service company have to fight and face the enemy with their bayonets?" Li Ma asked. Just like regular soldiers? I thought a special service company was supposed to stay with ranking officials and protect them. Like Jin Lizhi, isn't his duty to protect Taitai and Laoye?"

"When critical times call for it, they have to fight too, just like other soldiers! Haven't you ever heard Jin Lizhi talk about his battlefield experience?"

Li Ma persisted with her questions. "Will there be fighting at Daye?" After a moment she continued. "Is Jin Lizhi going there to fight?"

"Yes, he's going there to fight, to protect our nation!"

Still not satisfied with Taitai's answers, she remained standing quietly at Taitai's side, listening to her and Laoye discussing the war situation. It was all pretty much beyond her comprehension. There was talk about the Tian Family Village, and this and that village...

Li Ma walked away from the center of the courtyard; as she passed by the light of a lantern she suddenly experienced the sensation that she had grown larger, that she was filling the entire courtyard. It was as though she was exposed in all her nakedness before the eyes of the others. Like someone who had been discovered in the act of thievery, she quickly hid in the darkness. She was especially concerned with Wang the bodyguard, who was at that moment standing by Laoye's doorway, a toothbrush in his hand, seemingly brushing his teeth.

"That disgusting devil. What's he doing brushing his teeth in the dead of night..." she grumbled as she walked into the kitchen.

360 days in a year
Each of them a day of agonies
A life worse than the birds in the mountains
A life worse than the cicadas in the fields
A life worse than the birds in the mountains
A life worse than the cicadas in the fields

This was the tune Li Ma sang as she stood in front of the rice pot, alongside the water pipe and even beneath the clothes line. The drops of water that ran down from the knuckles on her coarse fingers spotted her trouser legs and her jade-blue cotton jacket. Shimmers of light danced on her bright red and slightly darkened lips, as though an oily beetle were concealed there.

Under the bright sun, the shade cast by the rosebush looked like it had been cut out of a piece of fabric; as though painted with a brush, it spread out, climbing over the laurel bush in front of the stone steps. On the twisting tips of the grape vine hanging down from the trellises were button-sized pale green grapes that looked like little glass beads; they moved slightly with each gust of wind.

If it had been a few days earlier, Li Ma would have touched the grapes or held them in her hand, and commented to anyone within earshot:

"They're almost ready to eat . . . so soon! How fast they've grown! . . ."

But now she didn't even notice them. As she passed by with a bamboo pole in her hand she unconcernedly knocked it against the grapevines, and the slowly undulating leaves continued to cast moving shadows on the ground long after Li Ma had passed by.

The sounds of her melancholy were not limited to that little tune, but could be discerned in the sounds of spoons, plates and bowls, for they had lost their crisp resonance. That melodic kitchen of days past, which had sounded like a music studio at the height of its activity, had now fallen into a sort of muted revery.

Some of the tender, white beansprouts still sported beards, but she fried them all together, beards and all. Rape and cabbage were thrown into the pan, still dripping with water, which sizzled in the pan. When they were served, a pale green, watery vegetable gravy spread out on the white plates.

She mopped her brow with her apron. The reflection in the mirror on the wall opposite her was of a frightened or a sick person; it reflected in her face the guilt and lonely look of a young mountain goat suddenly and recently abandoned at the height of its happiness.

Li Ma was only 25 years old. Her hair was still black, her skin taut and her heart that of a strong, healthy young person. The toes of her shoes were often split open owing to her habit of shuffling her feet as she walked. She was forever kicking the doorsill, the coal pile and the edge of the stone steps, although this didn't concern her. But the Li Ma whose reflection appeared in the mirror now was not the Li Ma of earlier days; it was a different person — dark, somber and silent.

After she had cleared the table, she walked away, saying: "I don't feel well... I've got a headache." She stood looking out beyond the lake with its calm waters, which had begun to grow a little choppy. Bees flitted to and fro on the powdery yellow flowers of the squashes, which were already climbing their way up the trellises. A large drop of water rested in the center of each of the plump, large lotus plants that covered the surface of the lake; they looked like drops of mercury shining under the sun. In the midst of the layer of plump, large leaves, light green, red-rimmed lotus blossoms stood out.

Some people were cutting down the grasses that grew on the banks of the lake so that they could have some greens with their meals. An old servant who worked in the landlord's home pointed over beyond the bamboo fence at the row upon row of steaming objects and said to Li Ma:

"Just look! Those soldiers are a pitiful lot. The wounded can't care for themselves and have to depend on their comrades to wash their things in the lake for them. Big blankets like those, you can never wash them clean. If you don't believe me, just take a look for yourself: they're rank and all smelly . . ."

She noticed some army blankets and faded olive drab military uniforms hanging across the bamboo fence on the west side of the lake. Li Ma knew that that was a military hospital, and she had grown to detest the place over the past few days. The sight of wounded soldiers on crutches threw a fright into her. She responded to the old man's comments with a hollow laugh. The men doing their washing on the bank of the lake were soldiers too; a dull sound of slapping water was created as they washed their clothes and beat them on the rocks.

"I've gone and forgotten to sew Jin Lizhi's leggings! I must be losing my mind. He'll be coming over to pick them up any minute."

By the time she had returned to the bank of the lake with needle and thread, a troop of soldiers was marching down the road on the other side, singing as they raised a cloud of dust. *Is Jin Lizhi in that group of soldiers?* The realization that she was on tenterhooks made her feel a little foolish.

Li Ma could sing all sorts of popular military songs, and every time she sang the familiar line, "When our Chinese nation faces its greatest danger," she unconsciously marched just like a soldier. She liked this particular tune a lot because it was one of Jin Lizhi's favorites.

But today she was disgusted by the sight of the soldiers, so she lowered her head and watched them out of the corner of her eye. The sounds of their singing were like those of little insects that swarmed around her at dusk — she couldn't escape them.

"Li Ma . . . Li Ma." The bodyguard named Wang was calling her, but she pretended she didn't hear him.

"Li Ma! Jin Lizhi's coming!"

She knew she was being teased. She walked over to the grassy spot in the center of the courtyard and stood there dumbly. Wang the bodyguard and Taitai were watching her.

"Li Ma, haven't you eaten yet?"

She twisted a legging in her hand. Her lips had turned purple and her eyes were fixed firmly straight ahead, although she wasn't staring at anything in particular. The other legging was lying flat out on the grassy ground at Li Ma's feet, slightly more yellow than its surroundings.

Jin Lizhi came that evening a little after eight o'clock, sporting an additional gold flower insignia on his red collar band; originally there had been two, and now there were three.

In Taitai's room, she had given him a glass of lemon tea in honor of his impending departure for the front lines.

"No tea for me, thanks. I just came here . . . I just came back to look around one last time. The company commander and I were out buying some things for the company. No tea for me, thanks . . . the company commander'll be here at eight-fifteen to see Laoye." He looked carefully at his wristwatch. "It's eight o'clock now, and as soon as the company commander comes, I'll have to be going back to the barracks with him . . ."

He began talking about going up to the front lines, where they were headed, what he would be doing there, what sort of person the special forces company commander was and how well he treated his men . . . he and Taitai chatted pleasantly. Li Ma picked up Taitai's cigarettes and offered one to Jin Lizhi.

"This time you're a guest. Here, smoke one of these!"

She ran outside to get the leggings, which she placed on the table. She picked them up and unrolled them, then rolled them back up again . . . she was as fidgety as a leaf drifting on a pool of wind-swept water.

Why doesn't he hurry up and come into the kitchen? Li Ma made a point of walking out of the room before the others, coughing twice by the side of the door as she did so. Then, in a loud voice, she began talking to the bodyguard Wang about things she didn't understand herself. Seeing that Jin Lizhi still hadn't come out, she went back into the room and said:

"Three gold flowers — just wait'll you come back

from the front lines, you'll probably have five of 'em.
Jin Lizhi's wearing a brand new uniform. Did they issue it to you?"

"Yeah," Jin Lizhi answered.

This wasn't the sort of answer Li Ma was looking for, so she said:

"It's five minutes after eight. Is Taitai's clock accurate?"

Taitai merely glanced over at the clock and nodded. She still hadn't gotten Jin Lizhi's attention.

"This time we'll be fighting for the nation. The company commander says that it's better to be the ghost of a fallen soldier than a nationless slave. For the sake of our fellow countrymen, our families and our children, we have to resist to the very end. . . ."

Jin Lizhi stood ramrod stiff as he chatted with Taitai.

Li Ma stole out of the room, stepped down off the porch, made a turn and headed out through the side gate. She had decided to buy him a couple of packs of cigarettes, recalling that cigarettes were a prize possession on a battlefield. As she ran down the lane she thought about what she wanted to say to him: "When you return all you have to do is find Laoye's official residence and that's where I'll be. Taitai says that she'll take me along wherever she goes." Then I'll remind him: "When you return don't forget me. Be sure you remain true to your word, and don't forget me when you get your promotions. . . ."

As she ran down the darkened lane she wasn't even aware that she was somewhat feverish. Then she remembered how it turned warm as soon as night fell, another example of the disagreeable Hubei weather. Her back was soaked with perspiration.

"I also have to give him this dollar. What good will it do me? Besides, I still have five dollars coming for next month's wages. But up on the front lines, money's limited. . . ." She fingered the dollar bill in her pocket.

By the time Li Ma returned, Jin Lizhi had long since departed down the lane — he was gone without a trace. She stood in the middle of the lane calling:

"Jin Lizhi . . . Jin Lizhi . . ."

Not a sound in response, not even the hollow echo that a shout produces in a mountain valley.

It was just like the time several years ago at home in Jiujiang, when she had sent another young man off to war. He had said that when his hitch was up he'd come back and marry her, and that everything would be fine. Just before leaving he had given her a bolt of cotton print material, the mere sight of which had brought her to tears afterwards. Now here she was, sending off this special forces soldier who told her that when the war of resistance was won he'd return and marry her, and that everything would be fine.

She also had to tell him: "I'll put my wages aside for the day when we set up housekeeping. Our own home."

But Jin Lizhi had already left. The company commander must have returned and taken him back to the barracks.

By the time this last thought had formed in her mind, a cool wind was caressing her spine as she stood there holding the cigarettes in her hand, like water being splashed against her. By then she was standing stock still and the heat of a moment before, as well as the highly charged and violent emotions she had been experiencing, had left her.

In that instant of hesitation and high emotion, life seemed to evaporate for her. Li Ma shivered, for people tend to feel chilled when they are motionless.

She turned to look at the pitch-black courtyard. She didn't feel like going back into it, but it was still preferable to the darkened small lane that stretched out before her.

Finally she turned and went back in, stumbling along the pale bricks of the roadway. The colors of the light from the lamp and the window curtains in the room were remarkably drab, giving them the appearance of a piece of cloth flapping in the air or a solitary ray of light amidst the darkness of the heavens. She opened the door leading to the female servants' quarters, walked in and sat down on her bed. It seemed to her that there were no insect noises this evening, that all about her was an unlimited emptiness; aimless rays of light spread out from the electric bulbs, the bedding was in complete disarray, the doors and windows were haphazardly placed . . . the total effect was that there was neither an orderly plan of existence in the world nor an orderly plan of extinction . . . .

She kept thinking about that last sentence she had been hoping to say; she would rather not have given it any more thought, but there it was:

"I'll put my wages aside for the day when we set up housekeeping."

Li Ma went to bed very early. This was the first time she had retired so early, long before any of the other female servants in the compound. Two packs of cigarettes lay beside her pillow.

Although it was already past dusk, the sounds of the soldiers singing on the banks of the lake could still be faintly heard.

That evening she dreamt that Jin Lizhi had returned from the front lines. "I've come back to set up a home for us. From now on, everything'll be fine." They'd won the war.

What's more, Jin Lizhi's hair was as black as it had always been.

"We had to win," he was saying. "How could we have lost? It doesn't make any sense."

Li Ma had a gentle smile on her face as she dreamt.

North China

A light snow was falling when people began to stir early in the morning. Standing beneath a gray-colored gateway nearby were two workmen in leather caps pulling hard on a two-man saw.

Twang! Twang! Twang! Twang! It sounded almost like a song, one that the shiny white saw sang the entire morning.

A large sawhorse stood beneath the gateway, across which had been placed a thick, round log some twelve inches or more in thickness and more than five feet in length. The two workmen were pulling their saw across the log, which, in no time at all, was cut in two. Once they had sawed it in half they cut each half into two more pieces. The cut pieces looked like small stools, some of which were standing on end, while the remainder were lying on their sides. Following that, another five-foot log was hoisted onto the sawhorse, where it too was promptly cut into two pieces, then four, all of which were similarly dumped onto the ground.

Another saw was being used a short distance away from the house. Just beyond the city gate was a wooded area, arranged not in the typical manner, but comprising a row of trees laid out on either side of a long narrow road. In former years, if any of the local peasants had stripped the bark off any of the elm trees that flanked this narrow road, they would, on orders of the owner, have been bound and horsewhipped. Stripping the bark from live trees is a sure way of killing them, and since these trees were said to be a hundred years old — they had been handed down by the present owner's ancestors — he was not about to let them be killed while they were under his care. He felt a responsibility to hand them down to his sons and grandsons, in hopes that they could stand as everlasting testimony to the greatness and splendor of his family.

But this year the trees were being cut down and sawed into sections, and on the orders of the present owner.

The trees were very, very old, and their roots ran deep into the ground; cutting the trees down was one thing, digging up the roots was quite another. So once the trees were downed, the decision was made to wait until the following spring before going after the roots.

Countless numbers of magpie nests, old and new, filled the branches, and as each tree crashed to the ground, the din was ear-splitting. The dry bark that had been assaulted by freezing northern winds shattered as it hit the ground. Then the magpie nests came raining down, some in pieces, others still in perfect condition, all of them settling into the glistening snow on the ground.

Those that broke upon impact were last year's nests, or perhaps even older. The others were new nests that had probably been made during the pervious summer to serve as the birds' home during the winter. They were as solid as could be, so even though they were lying on the ground with the trees, they were still in perfect condition and still anchored in the branches of the fallen trees. The feathers inside the nests looked nice and warm as they were blown about by the wind.

2

Bird hunting had always been prohibited in this wooded area, for the taking of any life was frowned upon. Children were not allowed to knock down or break up the birdnests either, for that was considered an immoral act — it would make the birds homeless.

But now not even the trees were standing.

No one knew just how long this row of trees had been there alongside the road, but it seemed as though they had stood as long as the place itself. This row of trees was the first thing you saw when you passed through the city gate, and that's how it had been for more years than anyone could remember. The people felt that the trees were a necessary feature of the place; now with the trees cut down, they walked out the city gate and immediately experienced a sense of desolation, like when you can't spot something you expect to see, or like when something is missing. Not all of the trees had been felled, but precious few remained by now.

So few of the original hundred or more elm trees still stood that they might as well have all been cut down. Now there was virtually nothing but a bunch of stumps, and from a distance they presented a queer sight. For all intents and purposes, all the trees were down. Since the final ten or so were in the process of being felled, the completion of the job was in sight.

One of the fur-capped workmen who were sawing the trees under the gateway said:

"What do you think of the chances that Da Shaoye* will ever return?"

"The way I see it," the other answered him, "he may not even be in the land of the living."

One of them removed his cap and dusted the frost off the earflaps, while the other removed a pipe from his waistband, for it was time to take a break.

Just then the front door of the main house opened resoundingly, and the old steward stepped out holding a red-bordered envelope in his hand. He had a hesitant look on his face and was biting his lower lip.

The two workmen, who were just about to light their pipes, could tell at first glance that the Master was causing trouble again. They both snatched the pipes out of their mouths, as one said to the other:

"Do you really think that Da Shaoye has gone to fight the Japanese?"

The old steward walked up to them, and after he had reached the gateway he sat down on the sawhorse and handed the envelope over for the others to look at. They were both illiterate, as, for that matter, was the old steward. But the latter could tell what was written on the envelope with his eyes closed, for the old Master had written one exactly like it every day from the very first day of his illness. Sometimes he wrote two a day, or three, or even as many as five, and he had been doing this for three months, the exact period of his illness.

---

* Literally, Eldest Young Master, or the eldest son of the family patriarch.

Even the children of the family knew what the envelopes said.

So the old steward held the envelope upside down between his fingers and read it:

To the Resistance Hero of the Great
Republic of China
My Son, Geng Zhenhua
from Your Father

The old steward's reading was flawless, except that in the middle line he had omitted the words "My Son" before the name Geng Zhenhua. One of the two workmen could hear that he had made a mistake, and was quick to correct him:

" 'My Son, Geng Zhenhua.' "

All three of the men looked the envelope over very carefully, but none could say with any certainty which of the words were "My Son"; that, of course, was because they were illiterate. But it really didn't make any difference, since all of them had the address down pat, so the steward tossed the envelope aside and they put it out of their minds. They began talking about the old Master — the man they worked for — and his illness. What, they wanted to know, was wrong with him. The traditional Chinese medicine practitioner had said that the fires in his liver were so strong that the resultant humour had laid him low, while the doctor trained in Western medicine had said that too much stress had caused a nervous breakdown. Then there was the famous local fortune teller, Huang Banxian, who had peeked in at the old Master through a crack in the door curtain and determined that in a previous incarnation he had been doomed to have his flesh torn from his bones.

Master Geng had left the county seat in the first year of the Republic (1912) to study in the provincial capital, and had come close to having the opportunity to study at Peking University. Although the opportunity had been missed, his thoughts were considered extremely revolutionary. He had hidden a photograph of Sun Yat-sen in one of his textbooks, which he finally dared to take out and show others around the year 1920. According to him, if he had been caught with this photograph before that time, his head would have rolled in the street.

So it can be said that he had the thoughts of a reformer, with a disdain for all superstition and no confidence whatsoever in Chinese medicine. He would not allow his son to be educated by private tutors, instead sending him and his brothers and sisters to a Western school as soon as they were old enough to be admitted.

His mother had been a very superstitious woman who believed in sorcerers and exorcism, but she was long-deceased. Now he was the undisputed head of the household, whose word was law. His wife, a woman in her fifties, had studied with a tutor. Her father had gone to Peking to sit for the examination during the Qing dynasty, and although he had not been successful, he was known as a man of learning. As a result, his daughter had mastered the *Diamond Sutra* and the Kitchen God prayer, and every night when silence reigned she burned incense, recited her prayers, and performed all her Buddhist devotions. Although she was already in her fifties, she had had to live under many restrictions from her husband, but she stuck to her guns, even burning incense at the altar of the Kitchen God when no one was looking.

Master Geng placed no stock at all in the Kitchen God or anything of that nature; once when he carelessly bumped into the Kitchen God's altar, he complained that he had been struck intentionally, so he had picked up the incense tongs and beaten the idol with them.

In answer to the question, "What is a god?" he said that man is a god. Ever since the advent of science, that which one could see existed, while that which one could not see did not exist — it was as simple as that.

And so when Huang Banxian poked his head in through the curtain, he was met by a stream of grumbling from the Master, who drove him from the room, making it necessary for the fortune teller to make his diagnosis through a crack in the curtain. Fortunately for him, he had great confidence in his own powers, so a brief look was all he needed to spot the problem. According to him, all of the Master's problems were fated from a previous incarnation: "True wealth cannot be taken away, a true son will not leave; true wealth cannot be taken away, a true son will not die." This was a popular old saying, although the part about the true son's leaving was a new twist that he had introduced, since no one knew whether Geng's eldest son was dead or alive. He thought it prudent to use the vague word "leave" to cover all possibilities.

If, for example, no news was received from the son because he was in fact dead, then the word "leave" was certainly appropriate. But if one day he returned, then "leave" would be the "leave" that alternated with "return" in life's ups and downs, as characterized in the saying, "sadness, happiness, leave, and return."

This theory of Huang Banxian's had to be kept under wraps, for even though Master Geng was gravely ill, he did have his lucid moments, and if he had caught wind of it, there would have been hell to pay in the home. He would have started his tirade with his wife and continued all the way down to the lowest kitchen servant. That was why all they could do openly during his illness was bring in a series of doctors and steer absolutely clear of all forms of witchcraft. So people like poor Huang Banxian were forced to come to the Mistress in her room with their hands out to get a little payment for their services. Time did not allow for any discussion of their prognosis.

At this time the two capped workmen took out their tobacco pouches and lit up. They both cleared their throats preparatory to embarking upon a weighty discussion of Da Shaoye's disappearing act. The old steward sat off to the side in possession of a rich storehouse of opinions. He stroked his beard, which, in the short time he had been there, had accumulated a coat of snow.

"I wonder if he's dead or alive," he mused. "It looks like we've lost one and will soon lose another"

One of the workmen asked him:

"Is the Master's illness any better?"

The old steward was sitting on the sawhorse, looking off in one direction then another with an expression of indifference on his face. It was hard to tell if he simply didn't care one way or the other or if there was something on his mind. The impression he gave was that the entire sequence of events was crystal clear to him, that he knew where things were headed, and that the outcome was never in doubt. He was like a man who could see into the future. He reached down and scooped up a handful of sawdust, then blew it into the air, scattering it all over himself. He brushed himself off until the sawdust had all fallen back to the ground, then bent down and picked up a wooden stick, which he placed onto the sawhorse, gave it a hit, and peeled off a strip of bark. He stuck the sliver of green bark into his mouth and began chewing on it as he said.

"It's still kinda sweet. Just think, a hundred-year-old tree has to meet its end today."

So saying, he kicked the piece of wood away as he commented:

"I've lived more than sixty years, but I've never lived through a year like this one. No one dares to disobey him. What he says goes. It's all over now."

The two workmen just stood there staring blankly ahead.

The old steward banged the bowl of his pipe against the sole of his felt shoe.

"When we were fleeing from the Russians, those big-nosed invaders went around butchering and slaughtering, but it was soon over and done with and they were gone. It was never like this: there isn't anything that escapes his attention — supplies, firewood, everything. He has to hear every word you say and read every word you write. Sure, you can say that the Master's illness is tied up with his son, but that's not the whole story; it's also tied up with the Japs."*

Just as he was saying this, two men in green uniforms, speaking a foreign tongue and wearing knives at their belts, walked up. The old steward reached out his foot and covered the envelope with the words The Great Republic of China written on it, which he had tossed to the ground. Nervousness showed on his face as he said:

"Been a lotta snow this winter! That means it's gonna be really green in the spring."

The two men walked off, leaving the scene as they jabbered back and forth in their foreign tongue.

"Speak of the devil!"

The old steward stood up and started walking back, picking up the envelope on his way; he tore it into shreds, stuffed the pieces into his mouth, and chewed them up before spitting them out as he made his way back to the house. Even when he had reached the steps of the main house, he could still be heard grumbling to himself:

"Nonsense, what nonsense, what goddam nonsense ..."

The door creaked as he opened it; then he walked into the house and disappeared from view.

Fresh snow continued to fall as the two workmen went back to work with their saw.

The sound of their saw had a singsong quality to it, but only when heard from a distance. The men using

---

* Although the last two characters have been deleted here, the context and the cautiousness of editors when this piece was published make the meaning clear.

the saw heard only the ripping sound of the teeth on wood.

The sawdust flew. A slightly sweet fragrance floated in the immediate area. It was a sweet but subtle aroma, neither the scent of pine nor willow, but one from the past that had been forgotten, only to reappear now after all these years, fresher than ever. The workmen occasionally scooped up a handful of sawdust, which they put into their mouths and swallowed. Before that they had chewed on pieces of green bark that they had stripped from the cut wood. It had the same fragrance and it freshened their mouths, so at first that was what they had used. Now even though they were no longer chewing the bark with which they felt such a bond, the stack of corded wood was a very appealing sight. From time to time they gave the logs a friendly slap or kick. Each time they sawed off a section, which rolled to the ground from the sawhorse, they would say:

"Off with you — go over there and lie down where you belong."

What they were thinking was that big pieces of lumber like this should be used to make tables or chairs or to repair a house or make window frames; wood like this was hard to find.

But now they were cutting it into kindling to be burned in stoves, a sad ending for good wood like this. They could see a comparison with their own lives, and this was a saddening thought.

The fresh snow fell like castoff shards of broken glass, leaving a trail of glitter on the men's faces and clothing. As they moved through the snow, the people looked as though they were enmeshed in a gauze net, one that was woven with threads of glass that floated in the air, scooted to and fro, and cascaded to the ground.

Looking through this into the gateway, the men's outlines were vaguely discernible, with no features — nose, eyes, anything — visible.

On the other hand, the noise of the saw carried farther and more clearly in the snowfall. That was partly because the inclement weather had forced most people indoors. The streets and courtyards were completely stilled — there were few human sounds to be heard and even fewer human shapes to be seen. There was virtually nothing but a white blur as far as the eye could see.

This was especially true in the wildwoods, where the white blur made the entire vista look like an enormous fossil. Anyone walking through the wildwoods far off in the distance resembled nothing more than a tiny black speck in motion. If the person were nearer, one could see little more than an outline moving through the haze.

The strangest phenomenon in a snowfall like this was that the nearer anything drew, the farther away it seemed to be. For example, if someone next to you was speaking, the sound was far less crisp than usual, but sounds coming from a great distance away seemed to emanate from right beside your ear. Which is why the two workmen could hear the sounds of other trees being felled so clearly whenever they stopped to rest.

The sound of the big saws was quite faint because of the distance — it sounded like it was coming from a faraway village and was filtered through several other villages along the way. It faded in and out, and if people forgot that trees were being felled out there, they would have been mystified by the sound. Either that or they wouldn't have heard it at all.

"More'n a hundred trees!" That was the original number and the number on their minds. . . .

On a clear day the row of trees would have been highly visible, but not during a snowfall — there was only the twanging sound of the saws. It was the sound that told them that trees were being cut down.

After listening for a moment, they said:

"More'n a hundred trees, and all of 'em will be burned to ashes. Master Geng's gone crazy thinkin' of his son."

Each year was worse than the previous. It was over, all over.

No more cherries appeared on the cherry trees, the rosebushes were barren. Mud walls collapsed, snapping cherry trees and burying rosebushes as they did. Branches from the broken cherry trees stood off at grotesque angles, the rosebushes were buried without a trace.

In earlier days Master Geng had asked the children:

"What are you going to do when you grow up?"

"Be an official," they had answered.

But those days were long gone.

Now what he said was:

"All you need is enough to eat and drink. We want nothing to do with a life of fame and riches."

The paintings of Wilson and Napoleon that used to decorate the living-room walls had been taken down. Napoleon had been a particularly heroic and majestic figure, with his imposing hat and the sword hanging at his side.

Every morning Master Geng had gone into the living room right after breakfast to sit and look at the paintings, starting with Wilson and Napoleon and moving on to Lincoln, Washington... They had hung in a neat line along the wall in a fixed order. After he had read off the names, his elder son would repeat them, then the younger son would point to each one, saying that this was Wilson, that was Napoleon...

Heroism and majesty had been important to him. To be manly, a real man, one should strive to be a Wilson or a Napoleon.

But all this had changed. The paintings had been removed and in their place had been hung a traditional painting of a quintessential righteous man standing very properly and composed in a wide-sleeved gown, his ears long and full, his lips a bright red. But from the very first day, the painting had hung there virtually without notice and unnamed.

He also stopped asking the children what they were going to do when they grew up, and on those infrequent occasions when the children broached the subject, he responded tersely:

"Worry about having enough food to eat and clothes to wear. Nothing else matters."

All of this dated from the day the Japanese had arrived, when his entire philosophy had undergone a change.

Sometimes he would say:

"Men live a hundred years, thirty-six thousand days, with less significance than half a day in the life of an idle monk."

Da Shaoye had still been living at home then. When he left, his father initially withheld all judgment, although anger filled his heart. In his view, his son was being extremely foolish. But he was sure that sooner or later he'd come to his senses and return home. Youngsters were attracted to all the exciting activity being talked about and wanted to see for themselves. Thinking back to his own youth, he recalled that he had been the same way: During Sun Yat-sen's revolution he had secretly joined the Revolutionary Party. But it wasn't quite the same anymore, for the youngsters nowadays were far more hot-blooded and yearned to fight the Japanese. Naturally, with all that fury in him it was best to let him go; he'd see the light in due time. He figured that by going south into China proper the boy was free of "Manchukuo" and could talk of fighting the Japanese. Actually, even there any talk of Resistance was strictly forbidden.

Two or three students from the local middle school had run off to join up, and it was rumored that they had been caught right after their arrival in Shanghai and had been accused of the seditious act of joining the Resistance. Now none of this may have been true, since Master Geng hadn't seen it with his own eyes, but he was inclined to believe it. As a man who loved his son dearly, he tended to believe any bad news that reached his ears. Now that his son had left, he thought, he was helpless to get him to come back home. His only hope was that the boy would return on his own when he ran up against trouble.

Just wait and see: he won't be in Shanghai more than a few days before he'll be back home again. That's what young people are like these days — they're fast to fall in with anything that sounds exciting, but it never lasts more than a few days.

So Master Geng didn't put much stock in the whole affair.

As for the boy's mother, she cried nonstop for three or four days. She said that three or four days before he had left, she had spotted something unusual in him — his eyes were all red from crying, showing his impatience to leave.

"Ma," he had said to her "you should make Younger Brother and the others study Chinese lessons a couple of hours a day. Now all they see is Japanese books, and someday they may forget their Chinese altogether. When we finally drive the Japanese from our shores, just think of the shame when our own young people can speak nothing but Japanese!"

"When are we going to drive the Japanese from our shores?" she had asked in return.

"I'm getting ready to do my part."

He couldn't have given a clearer indication of his intentions, but unfortunately she had missed the significance. Now she could kick herself whenever she thought back to that time.

If she had been more alert she could have stopped him from going — she could have kept him there if only she had been more alert. She could kick herself, for now he might never return.

Although she did not see the necessity of resisting the Japanese, now that her son had left, she feared that he might never return home. Where this dark thought came from she had no idea; possibly the fact that no news had been received from the two local middle-school students after their arrival in Shanghai had terrified her. Whatever the reason, her heart was gripped by foreboding, as though her son had left home, never to return again.

She didn't tell anyone what was in her heart, nor did

she even have a desire to. But her foreboding increased the more she thought about it. That was why she broke into tears at the sight of her son's hunting cap as she was tidying up his room, and why she cried when she saw his leather gloves, her flow of tears virtually unending.

She neatly stacked his books on his desk, put his writing brushes into the holder, and his pencils into the pencil box. His glass was still half filled with tea. How could she accept the fact that her son was gone! His wristwatch was lying on the bookcase, still ticking off the seconds. His very own wristwatch!

She touched this thing and that, moved one thing or another. Nothing seemed to be missing, it was all there. The room was still warm, just as though it were waiting for her son to come home at night and sleep there as always. It was ludicrous to think that this room's occupant had gone, never to return!

3

Their son had now been gone for three years. He had sent them a grand total of two letters from Shanghai, and that was the last they had heard from him, although several reports of him did reach them. In fact, there were so many rumors that they didn't know which to believe. He hadn't been gone six months before the July 7, 1937 Marco Polo Bridge Incident and the attack on Shanghai slightly more than a month later occurred, and China was formally at war with Japan. But still they didn't know where their son was. One rumor had it that he had joined up with the forces of General

Zhang Fakui in Shanghai. Another said that he was not a soldier, but was engaged in political work. Later on one of his schoolmates said that he had long since left Shanghai and was working for the Eighth Route Army in Shaanxi. A few months later all these reports were denied, and it was said that he was employed as an elementary-school teacher in Shanxi. The most farfetched rumor of all said that he had fallen on such hard times that he had become a down-and-out vagabond and had been forced to hire on as a temporary laborer in a ceramics factory.

This rumor had come as a real blow to his mother, who had searched high and low for any news of him: she had sought out his relatives, friends, and anyone who had ever known him to find out what they knew. She had paid particular attention to his schoolmates, for to her way of thinking, since they were young themselves, they must have heard from him. When they told her that they honestly didn't know a thing, she would say to them: "You're not telling me the truth. How could he not write to you?"

She had wanted to send him some money, but she didn't know where to send it. She didn't have a single address for him.

She was of the opinion that someone knew her son's whereabouts, but that no one dared tell her. She was especially convinced that his schoolmates knew, but were unwilling to say so. They were afraid that as soon as they told her, she'd go and bring him back. That's why she was always saying to them:

"Please tell me if you know. You have my word I won't go and bring him back."

At other times she'd say:

"I think it's good for him to go out and see the the world. I don't know anyone else from the three Northeastern provinces who's ever been to Shanghai. He's over 21, so it's his business if he wants to fritter his life away in some faraway place. I wouldn't go and bring him back even if I knew where he was."

But the response was always the same:

"We don't know where he is, we really don't."

Sometimes her impassioned pleas captured the sympathy of her listeners:

"Old Auntie, we honestly don't know. If we did we'd tell you."

The result was always the same — she came away empty-handed, and it always left a void in her heart. She vowed never to ask anyone again, no matter who, since no one gave a damn anyway. They were a bunch of selfish people. She grew to hate them all because they wouldn't tell her, and she was determined never to ask again.

But her resolve invariably melted after a few days, and she was soon asking around again.

How could he have become a common laborer? No one in the Geng family, since way back to our ancestors, had ever been a hired hand. It must have been a joke, and she refused to believe it. It didn't seem possible.

But then she hadn't sent him a red cent since he left home, and with no family in Shanghai, there might have been some truth in the rumor after all.

She loved her son so much that this thought disturbed and saddened her, usually resulting in tears. Her son had been proud and indignant ever since childhood; all of his needs — food, clothing, everything — had been taken care of by someone else, so how could he possibly adapt to the life of a common laborer? My poor little boy! If her thoughts took this direction while she was eating, she would lose her appetite and lay down her ricebowl. If she was about to fall asleep at night, these thoughts would snap her awake, leaving her to toss and turn the rest of the sleepless night. If there was a strong wind outside, she would think of someone all alone out in the wind, unable to sleep and homesick, and she would feel terrible.

With thoughts of her son on her mind, she assumed that his thoughts were of home.

During a sound sleep one rainy night a peal of thunder woke her with a fright and kept her awake the rest of the night. She wondered how anyone far from home and penniless could possibly sleep on a windy, rainswept night like this. Adrift far away from home, with neither family nor friends to rely upon, and faced with wind and rain — how sad! Actually, for all she knew, he may have been thousands of miles away, where tonight's rain could never reach him. She merely assumed that when it rained on her it had to also be raining on him, wherever he was.

The reports that he had become a laborer or a soldier were nothing more than unsubstantiated rumors. As a result, she passed two or three years as though in a trance. She was like a woman who had lost her way, not knowing which way to turn.

During these three years, she was barely able to function. Whenever she heard someone singing a drum song she broke into tears; the same thing happened when she entertained children with a tall tale. As she told them about a beggar who had starved to death on the street after going without food for three days, she wondered why no one had been willing to give him some leftovers. Tears began to fill her eyes as she talked of people's heartlessness.

She didn't know why she was so quick to cry these days, sometimes for no good reason. She cried at the drop of a hat — at weddings, when she saw someone holding a grandchild, and even if she heard that so-and-so had announced his engagement.

4

Master Geng was a different matter altogether. He was absolutely closed-mouthed about it all: he never mentioned his son, he never cried, and he never spoke. The only effect on him was nearly total insomnia. He would just sit quietly, often all night long. He sat in front of a candle, an unopened book alongside him. He had never read a single page of the book, which merely lay beside him, keeping him company every night in the dim candlelight.

Shortly after his son's departure he assumed that the boy would be back soon, so there was no reason to be concerned. His reaction to the sight of his wife crying was: "Women have too many tears!" So when his son wrote home for some money, not only did he refuse to send any, he even wrote back to tell him that if he came home, everything would be all right, but if he didn't, then he'd have to fend for himself and could forget about writing any more letters home. After all, it was a capital offense to correspond from one side of the Great Wall to the other. He took this position to intimidate his son and expedite his return. The last thing he had expected was that his son would read the letter and break off all communications with his family from then on.

Three years passed without a word, and even though many rumors came to him, they eventually got so depressing that he stopped listening. He hardened his heart and carried on as though he had never had a son like that. Some of the rumors reached his ears despite his efforts, but since they were all unsubstantiated, he had to treat them like the intermittent strains of a stringed instrument, listening as patiently and as discriminatingly as possible.

In order to put the matter out of his mind once and for all, he took to staying awake all night long and just sitting there.

After three years of sitting through the night, his hair turned completely white.

At first, friends and relatives asked whether or not he had heard from his son, but they stopped asking, since their questions prompted an angry response from him: "Why don't they mind their own business!"

Everyone was aware that he assiduously steered clear of any mention of his son, so his family avoided the subject like poison. He had the door to his son's room sealed, and from then on the room was deathly silent and soon covered with a layer of dust. The windows were so dirty that you could see your reflection in them when the sun shone from behind — it was like looking into quicksilver. The only way you could see the bed, bookcases, desk, and other items in the room was to flatten your nose up against the window, but even then you couldn't see very clearly; the layer of dust on the window blurred everything inside.

Virtually no one dared to even try to look through the window; the exception was the old steward, who, owing to his forgetfulness, suffered the angry stares of Master Geng more than once. On some days he would sneak a look through the window twice, once in the morning and once at night. That was because the departure of Da Shaoye had left the old steward with the feeling that the house was empty, or that death had visited the home, leaving an air of desolation in its wake.

It was obvious that the departure of Da Shaoye had taken the life out of the family. At mealtime the bowls were set out, but no one came to the table to use them. At bedtime no one slept. Throughout the house lamps were lit as the residents sat up all night long. No one paid any attention to kitchen supplies, so the old cook had a free hand to pilfer all the oil and salt he wanted; he even filled a sack with rice and walked off with it. No one checked the figures when firewood or grain supplies were delivered; the firewood was stacked carelessly onto the woodpile, the grain was just dumped into the storage bins. Whether the quantity was accurate or not no one knew.

If part of the fence collapsed, it was crudely propped up with grain stalks; if a roof leaked, the hole was plugged with a brick. Deterioration was setting in fast. Da Shaoye had walked off, taking the life-blood of the family with him.

In the eyes of the old steward, the home was in the throes of a fatal decline, which caused him unspeakable anguish.

He had been around during the previous generation and had seen Master Geng's father work conscientiously to make something of the family. Now where had it all gone? It looked to him as though everything were about to go up in smoke.

The more he looked around, the crazier it all seemed, and the more he felt like looking around. Since he figured there was no one around, he tiptoed up to Da Shaoye's window and looked inside. He had no idea what he was looking for; maybe he was just being nostalgic.

None of Master Geng's other children dared to even mention their brother's name, for anyone who did was met with an angry glare from his father. If one of them let the name slip out during mealtime or at play, his father would say:

"Go on, go somewhere else and play."

Master Geng seldom spoke any longer. He just sat in his room staring straight ahead at the wall with his gray eyes. If he was standing in the yard he stared up at the sky. He said nothing and looked at nothing in particular. If his jaw had been set any more tightly, one would have thought that he was biting down on something.

5

But now Master Geng was suffering from a nervous disorder that found him alternating between periods of alertness and a trance-like sleep.

His condition dated from December of the lunar calendar, when news of his son's probable death reached him.

This news had been passed on by one of his son's schoolmates who lived on the same street.

It was at this very time that the "Manchukuo" newspapers were running headlines of an imminent civil war in China and a cessation of hostilities with Japan. They reported that a certain Chinese military unit had attacked and wiped out another Chinese unit, including the soldiers' wives and children.

This propaganda by the Japanese was anything but well intentioned, proof of which appeared below the headline, where the readers were told of the fine qualities of "Manchukuo" and reminded of the prosperity of the nation and the happiness of her people; the Japanese denied having any designs on the fatherland of the Chinese people.

One glance was all Master Geng needed to convince him that the Japanese were trying to stir up trouble.

He read the papers every day, and although he didn't believe what he read, it did no harm to be aware of what they were saying; besides, it was a good way to pass the time. One day he spotted a drawing of several small figures, which bore the caption, "Killing one another." Another illustration, a group of Japanese leading some people from "Manchukuo", was captioned "Japanese and Manchukuo citizens walking hand in hand."

When he finished that day's newspaper, he snorted:

"The Japs will never subjugate China. They're a shameless people!"

One day while he was eating, a young man came into the living room, speaking in a subdued voice. After he had had his say he left. Master Geng seemed to be completely unaware that something was going on in the living room.

Mrs Geng was also eating at the time and when she realized that someone had come to their living room, she left the table and never returned to finish her meal.

By that evening everyone in the household knew, but they all kept the news from the Master. Da Shaoye had been killed in battle in some faraway place.

The old steward took a lantern to the temple, where he burned incense. When he returned, his beard was soaked with tears.

"He was so young," he said, "too young to die. Such a well behaved, mannerly boy, so warm and refined...."

One of the fur-capped hired hands said over and over:

"It's strange, real strange. Soldiers are usually poor people. Why would someone like Da Shaoye want to be a common soldier?"

One of the others had the answer:

"To fight the Japanese!"

The hired hands were talking among themselves in the servants' kitchen. A small kerosene lamp had been lit and placed on the stove, and since it had no shade, black smoke rose from it like a chimney. Hogfeed was cooking noisily in a pot on the stove, sending clouds of steam upwards, where it cooled then dripped from the rafters. A steady pitter-patter of condensed steam accompanied the sound of the men discussing Da Shaoye.

Mrs Geng had a good cry in her room, then picked up three sticks of incense and went up into the attic to kneel and recite the *Diamond Sutra*. The tips of the burning sticks of incense in her hand flickered from side to side as she walked through the darkness. Finally the red glows halted in the attic.

The old steward stood guard for her like a sentry, making sure that her husband stayed in his room. She fell to her prayers in earnest, her recitations mixed with sobs that soon turned into wails; as the volume increased, the old steward warned her:

"Not so loud — the Master might hear!"

She forced herself to hold back as best she could, resulting in an occasional stifled sob that made her sound as though there were something caught in her throat.

After she had finished her prayers, she walked back to her room in a daze. She was surprised to see her husband's reflection in the mirror when she got there. She assumed that he had seen everything and knew exactly what was going on, so when he asked her what she was doing, she decided to tell all:

"Our son's been killed by the Chinese."

"Nonsense!" he snorted.

He picked up a stack of newspapers and stayed up half the night reading them. They were filled with reports on all the discord the Japanese were sowing, but not a word about Chinese fighting their fellow countrymen.

Daybreak found him slumped over at his desk, his head pillowed by the stack of newspapers; he was having a dream.

His son was still very much alive in this dream — he was a Resistance hero, a leader of thousands of troops from China proper who were fighting their way north to "Manchukuo".

6

Master Geng's illness began as soon as he awoke from his dream; from then on he alternated between periods of a dazed trance and alertness.

During his lucid moments he would point to the trees being cut down and say:

"Cut them down! I'd be a sucker not to."

When the trees had been cut up into small sections he ordered:

"Burn them! I'd be a sucker not to. I won't let the Japs have 'em."

When he was in his trance-like state he would ask for his brush and some ink to write letters. How many he wrote no one will ever know, and all of them consisted solely of an envelope with nothing inside.

Each and every envelope looked the same:

> To the Resistance Hero of the Great
> Republic of China
>
> My Son, Geng Zhenhua
>
> From Your Father

Even he had no idea where these letters were to be sent, but whenever he had a visitor he would say:

"Wait a moment, would you send a letter for me?"

If the old steward was headed into town with an empty bottle to buy some wine, he would be stopped as he passed by the Master's window:

"Wait a moment, I've got a letter here I want you to send."

No matter who it was, if he spotted someone going into town he asked him to send a letter for him.

When the doctor came, before he even had time to lay down his medical bag, he would be asked by the old man:

"Wait a moment, would you mind sending a letter for me?"

His family was frightened by all of this, for if the visitor happened to be Japanese, they knew what would happen when the old man asked him to send a letter addressed to a Resistance hero.

That was why they confined him to his room — a back room in the last building at the rear, outfitted with a door curtain in front and shutters on the rear window — almost from the first day of his illness.

On clear days the room was filled with pale yellow sunlight, while on overcast days it had a gray cast to it. The room was virtually empty; with the exception of a huge firewall made of white porcelain wall tiles, which stood off to one side, all the furniture had been removed. The firewall was a permanent fixture, so it had to remain there for Master Geng's unhurried scrutiny. He seemed not to even recognize it, as though its nature was completely foreign to him. Sometimes he just looked at it, at other times he ran his hand over the tiles.

His family had been so frightened by his behavior that they had moved everything else out of the room. Otherwise he would have subjected everything to the same intense scrutiny; he would have inspected them all — lamp tables, teacups, plates, hatboxes, everything.

Now it was all gone, all but the firewall, which could not be moved. So he spent his time tracing the patterns on the firewall with his hand, saying from time to time:

"I'll bet this is Japanese-made!"

He passed his days in unrelieved boredom.

All day long the curtain hung limp in the doorway and the window shutters remained in place. He passed his days in semi-darkness, completely cut off from the outside world.

His room was quiet inside, but he could still hear outside noises; if he heard the bark of a dog or someone's footsteps, he would say:

"Let me go outside and take a look. Someone's coming." Or:

"Someone's coming. I want him to send a letter for me."

If anyone barred his way, he put up no resistance. But if there was no one around, he walked out the door, passed through Mrs Geng's bedroom and the living room, and went outside.

One day a Japanese representing the board of directors of some Japan-East Asia mutual benefit association came to the house to discuss something with Master Geng, who was also a member of the board.

Poor Mrs Geng received the scare of her life that day.

"He went into town," she said, her face a ghostly white.

She was petrified that she'd say the wrong thing, for if the man knew that her husband was ill at home and could receive no visitors, the whole affair might be out in the open. They could be accused of any number of irregularities.

Afterwards they had a family meeting, where they decided to move Master Geng to another place. His new room was small and chilly. It was a sideroom originally occupied by a serving girl; it had no heater or firewall and was warmed only by a small charcoal brazier. Since it was the last room at the rear of the compound, it should have fitted their needs perfectly.

But that's not how it worked out. The doctor came by one day to look in on Master Geng, and as he was telling the rest of the family in the living room that there was no change in the patient's condition, Master Geng parted the door curtain and walked in with an envelope in his hand.

"I'm fine, just fine. Would you please send this letter for me?"

Mrs Geng was thrown into a panic, for if their visitor had been Japanese, they would have been in deep trouble. So they moved him again, this time to an even more remote spot in the compound — an enclosed arbor in a corner of the garden.

Just like a little Buddhist shrine, the arbor had hanging chimes at each corner, which clinked together as they rustled in the night winds.

During his lucid moments, Master Geng would say:

"I never thought I'd leave home and become a monk. That makes me laugh!"

But when he was in his trance-like state, he said:

"Give me my brush, I want to write a letter...."

People seldom came out to the garden, especially during the winter, when it was blanketed with snow. On rare occasions a stray dog would cut across the garden, leaving a trail of paw prints in the snow, thereby breaking the symmetry and destroying the pristine beauty of the snow-covered ground that seemed almost sacred in its purity. It was a disturbing sight, which remained until the next snowfall, even if that was eight or ten days later.

Out on the street footprints in the snow were ignored by everyone; for that matter, a kitten's paw prints on a table were generally overlooked, like the path of a bird flying overhead. But not with this snow-covered flat ground; every hollow, every speck piqued the curiosity of observers. The prints of a mouse that had scurried across the snow looked like pairs of date pits that had been tossed onto the ground.

When a chicken crossed over this piece of land it left behind prints that reminded one of pine branches. Anyone seeing them automatically wondered where the chicken had come from and where it was headed. If the prints went a short way then turned abruptly and headed in the opposite direction, it was clear to the observer that the animal hadn't gone very far in the snow before turning back. Sometimes the prints went on and on in a straight line, all the way to the wall, or to one of the tall trees, or to the enclosed arbor, or even farther, beyond the observer's range of vision.

This small snow-covered piece of ground was bordered on all four sides by a high wall; undisturbed, it was a little world unto itself, but the addition of prints in the snow made it seem much larger. Any dog that had left its prints behind had to have left the area by jumping over the wall or running through one of the gates; a careful look revealed that the prints ran in a single straight line, showing that it had been a one-way journey.

From the day he was moved into the arbor, Master Geng did little but sit and stare at the snow-covered ground. Following a fresh snowfall, the ground was perfectly level, and during those times, when not a single blemish appeared in the snow, he felt lonelier than usual.

During these lonely times, he added charcoal to the brazier that heated his arbor, then sat down and stared long and hard at the blue smoke that rose to the ceiling.

7

Two relatives came to call on Master Geng one day; they were more than a little anxious that the sight of them would trigger his desire to write another letter to "The Great Republic of China Resistance Hero, My Son, Geng Zhenhua".

So instead of going inside to see him, they just walked around the arbor, stepping on the snow, with the idea of sneaking a look at him through the window.

But they couldn't see him — there wasn't a trace of him anywhere.

This news flustered Mrs Geng, who was convinced that he had sneaked out when no one was looking. But where could he have gone? God forbid he'd gotten himself into some sort of trouble! She hurried up the steps, noticing when she reached the door that it was still securely sealed with the lock that she had placed on it the last time she had left the place. Feeling greatly relieved, she assumed that he must be sleeping. Asking the visitors to wait outside the door, she decided to enter the arbor. If he was lucid, she would invite them in, but if not, she'd ask them to come back another time, avoiding the possibility that her husband would start in again with his letters to the Great Republic of China. But when she put her ear to the door she was sure she could hear his heavy breathing inside, so she told her visitors that he was asleep and that they should let him sleep a while longer. She walked back to the main house with them, chatting as she went.

When the cook took the Master's meal out to him, he opened the door and was met by a blast of bluish smoke, which filled the room. He spotted the Master lying on the floor beside the charcoal brazier, one hand resting on his chest, looking as though he was asleep. He also had the appearance of someone who had left a great many things unsaid.

Master Geng had been asphyxiated by smoke from the burning charcoal.

The chimes at the four corners of the arbor were clinking in the wind.

The light wind was a sign that it was about to snow.

Spring in a Small Town

IN the third lunar month the fields are already turning green. Mossy-looking patches appear everywhere. The grass in the fields has to make several twists before it bores through to the surface. Broken seed husks still dangling on their tips, green blades more than an inch long push up cheerily from the ground. When a child pasturing an ox happens to pick up a fallen tile at the foot of someone's wall and finds a bit of grass under it, he's sure to tell his mother when he gets home: "I saw grass today, Mama!" And Mama, pleasantly surprised, replies: "It must have been a place in the sun!" White *jianggeng* grass seeds roll along like round white stones, and country children collect them by the score. Dandelions begin to sprout, sheep bleat, ravens circle round the poplar trees. The weather keeps getting warmer; slowly the days grow more interesting. Poplar seed fluff fills the air and covers the ground like cotton. Everyone keeps catching it in their hands, and it sticks to them all over. Hay and cow dung strewn upon the road give off a pungent aroma. In the distance hollow thuds can be heard as children fling stones against the sides of boats beached upon the shore.

The ice on the river has broken. Chunk upon chunk strain laboriously, break off, then float rapidly downstream. Ravens standing on the blocks of ice watch for little fish, or frogs still in their winter sleep.

Suddenly the weather gets very warm. It's the first flush of spring. Of course it will turn cold again, but these few days are warm indeed. Spring with its powerful call roves over the land. . . .

Poplar fluff covers the small town. It flies in every street and lane, dropping like snowflakes even before the elms become yellow-green. . . .

Spring has come. It's as if an outburst which everyone has been long awaiting is going to explode this very night. Guiltily, all want to take part in this try for freedom. . . . Spring breathes at the threshold of every person's heart, calling, beguiling. . . .

A maternal aunt of mine was probably in love with one of my cousins.

A maternal aunt is a very close relative — a mother's sister. But this aunt wasn't my real aunt. She was the daughter of my step-mother's step-mother. Of course she could have been a partial blood relative of my step-mother, but she wasn't. For her mother was a widow when she married my maternal grandfather and Jade, my aunt, was a child of her previous marriage.

Jade had a sister who was two years younger, probably seventeen — which made Jade around nineteen.

Though not especially pretty, Jade was slender and had a serene lovely walk. Her speech was clear and charged with quiet emotion. When she stretched out a hand to take some cherries, her fingers touched them lightly, pityingly, as if afraid to hurt them.

If she were walking and someone behind her called, she would stop. If she were eating, she would first put down her bowl, then turn her head and look over her shoulder, moving her body only slightly. And she would deliberately bring her lips together, as if there were something she wanted to say but didn't know how to put it at the moment. . . .

Her younger sister, on the other hand — I forget what her name was — loved to talk and laugh, and wasn't very neat. Sister was the exact opposite of Jade. She'd buy any gaudy material, so long as it was popular on the market, have it quickly made into a gown and wear it. As soon as she had it on, she'd go around visiting her relatives. If anyone praised the material, she always said she had given another piece just like it to her sister Jade.

There weren't any other girls my own age in my maternal grandfather's household. Whenever I went there, Jade's mother used to call her over to play with me.

Jade lived in a rear court that was separated from the rest of the compound by a wooden wall. She came when she heard us call. Because there was no door through the wall, she had to go out into the street and walk around to our front gate.

Sometimes she would first greet me through one of the cracks in the wall, then go back to her room and dress up a bit before making her way through the street to her mother's chambers.

She was very fond of me. Since I had been studying in school and she had not, she thought I knew more than she about everything. She liked to discuss her problems with me, and get my opinions.

When I stayed over at grandfather's, she would spend the night with me.

We would talk from the moment we got into bed, far into the night. Somehow we could never finish. . . .

We'd start by discussing how clothes should be worn, what colors they should be, what material. Or whether a girl should walk slowly or quickly. Or if Jade had bought a brooch that day she would take it out and look at it, and ask me whether I really thought it was nice. In those days — it must have been fifteen years ago — we didn't know how girls in other places dressed, but in our town nearly everyone had a big woollen shawl which she wore draped over her shoulders. They were all colors, blues and purples, but the most by far were date-red. You saw practically nothing but date-red shawls out on the street.

Even though there were plenty of reds and greens, date-red was certainly the most popular color.

Sister had one, Jade had one, and so did almost all my classmates. Even my unfashionable grandmother wore a shawl across her shoulders, only hers was blue. She didn't dare use the popular date-red. After all she was an older woman. She felt she ought to let the younger women shine.

It also became fashionable at the time to wear shoes with woollen uppers. Sister went right out and bought a pair. A crude, careless girl, she didn't care whether the shoes were any good or not. If others had them, she had to have them too. Other girls wore their clothes — Sister dressed so sloppily her clothes seemed to be wearing her. But she stuck to the principle of buying whatever she felt she ought to have.

Sister put on the woollen shoes she had bought and began running around in them on the wooden floor. It wasn't long before the pompon on one of the shoes became loose. It jumped around, hanging on to the shoe by a single thread. It was very comical, like a big red date tied to her foot — her shoes were also date-red.

Everyone laughed at her for buying a pair of shoes that went bad the moment she brought them home.

Jade didn't buy any, though she thought about it a long time. No matter what new thing came on the market, she was never very quick to buy. Perhaps she liked them from the start, but she gave the appearance of being unimpressed, as though she couldn't possibly consider them.

Only after a great many people bought a thing would she show a little interest.

Like the question of buying shoes with woollen uppers. One night she and I discussed them, and she asked me what I thought. I said they were good looking, that many of my classmates had bought them.

The next day Jade asked me to go shopping with her. She didn't tell me what she wanted to buy. When we went into a shop she spent a long time picking over various other things before asking to be shown some woollen shoes.

We tried several shops, but none of them had any. They said they were all sold out. Shop-keepers all have the same tricks. They pretend their shop always has the best stock in town — they just happen to be out of the thing you want. I told Jade that we should take our time; other shops were bound to have them.

From Grandfather's house at the end of the road we had taken a carriage to the center of town.

We had got out at the first shop we saw. Needless to say, we had already paid the driver. After finishing our shopping we intended to hire another carriage, since we didn't know how long we would be. Probably if we saw some nice things we'd buy a few, even though we didn't need any. Or we might linger a while at a counter, although we had already made our purchase and there was no need to linger any more. Or, although the original purpose of our trip had been to buy a pair of shoes, we would end up not buying shoes but going home with a lot of other things we didn't need at all.

That day we dismissed the carriage and entered the first shop. It may not have been like that in the bigger cities, but in our small town that's the way it was: Even though you paid the driver and told him to look for other fares, he often waited at the door of the shop so that when you came out he could ask you to ride in his carriage again.

We entered the first shop. They said they had no woollen shoes. Then we looked at some other things, from silks and satins to wool serges, from wool serges to silks and satins. We didn't even glance at ordinary cotton cloth. It wasn't at all the way our mothers shopped — buying a length of this for a bed sheet, a length of that for a padded tunic. We had nothing to do with such matters. Our mothers wouldn't see the inside of a shop for a month at a time, but when they did it was a case of this is cheap, let's buy it, that's not costly, we'll take some of that too. For instance they might buy a colored cotton summer print in winter because it was cheaper then — sooner or later they'd be able to put it to use. But we weren't like that. We went shopping every day, hunting for pretty things, expensive valuable things, things for which we had absolutely no use, things we had never even thought about.

That day we bought a lot of fancy trimmings, some decorated with sequins, some with glass beads. We couldn't have told you what kind of gowns we were going to make in order to be able to use these trimmings. Perhaps we hadn't actually thought of making any clothes. We just bought the trimmings on impulse, saying they were beautiful. Jade said they were beautiful, and so did I. But later when we got home and opened up our packages for everyone to see, and this one criticized this and that one criticized that, we weren't quite so sure. Half the edge was taken off our enthusiasm. So we snatched the trimmings back from people's hands and quickly wrapped them up again, saying they didn't recognize value, that we wouldn't let them look.

We announced with an effort:

"We're going to make gowns of red-gold velvet and trim them with these black beads."

Or:

"This red trim we're going to send someone as a gift. . . ."

Although this is what we said, we weren't at all sure. Probably from this moment on, the things we had thought so adorable would never again see the light of day.

In our small town there weren't, after all, many shops. So when we couldn't find any woollen shoes, we got worried. No doubt we walked more quickly, for in a short time only two or three shops remained. And these were precisely the shops we seldom patronized. They were small, and didn't have much stock. We were sure they wouldn't have what we were looking for.

We went into one of them. Although they had three or four pairs, those that weren't too small were too big. And their colors were all ugly.

But Jade seemed to be considering them. I was surprised. She hadn't been so keen on the shoes in the first place. Since the shop didn't have any good ones, why should she want them? After I spoke to her, she decided not to buy, and we went home.

Two days later I had forgotten completely about woollen shoes.

But Jade suddenly proposed that we shop for some.

Then I knew her secret. She had fallen in love with those woollen shoes. She just hadn't admitted it, that was all. Jade wanted to take the secret of her love to the grave, never breathing a word, as if in all the world there was no one worthy of being entrusted with it. . . .

Wrapped in a fur rug, Jade and I rode in a carriage through a heavy snowfall to buy shoes with woollen uppers. The driver, sitting high on the platform on top, rocked as he sang a ballad in a hoarse voice. The wind whistled in our ears. Big thick snowflakes danced before our eyes. The horizon was a blurry mist. I silently prayed that Jade would soon get her darling shoes. From my heart I wanted her to be saved. . . .

The buildings of the market center stood hazily in the distance. Very few people were abroad. The streets were shrouded in silence. As we inquired from door to door, I was more agitated than Jade. I wanted her to buy the shoes quickly. I carefully questioned all the salesclerks, not willing to abandon the slightest clue. I encouraged Jade. I didn't forget a single shop. My enthusiasm must have surprised her a bit. But I paid no attention to her wonderment. I put everything into finding her a pair of shoes with woollen uppers in that small town of ours.

Our carriage, because Jade's hopes were riding with it, rolled along the streets with special verve and speed.

The snow was falling more heavily now. The streets were deserted except for the two of us, hurrying our driver — go here, go there. We tried until very late in the day. But there were no shoes to be had. Jade gave me a significant look and said: "I'm not fated to have a good destiny." I wanted desperately to act grown-up and say something to comfort her. But before I could think of anything suitable, tears gushed from my eyes.

2

Afterwards Jade often came to stay at our place. My step-mother invited her. Her younger sister had become engaged. We were afraid that when she married and Jade was left alone, it would make Jade unhappy. They didn't have many people in their household. Only an old grandfather, over sixty, and a widowed aunt and her daughter.

Of course her cousin should have been able to play with her and relieve her loneliness, but their temperaments were too far apart. They could no more mix than fire and water.

I saw the girl. She always wore somber clothes and had a dark complexion. From morning till night she sat with her mother in their room. When the mother washed clothes, she also washed clothes. When the mother wept, she wept too. Perhaps she was helping her mother cry for her departed father. Perhaps they were crying because their family was poor. No one knew.

Although they all were part of the same big family, whereas this girl looked like an ordinary country bumpkin, Jade and her sister behaved like pampered daughters of the rich. It was this which earned Jade the right to come and stay at our house frequently.

A year after she became engaged, Sister got married. During that year she was very well off, because the boy's family gave her marriage gifts as soon as the engagement was announced. In our town they didn't use government currency but notes issued by a private bank, equivalent to one hundred or one thousand coppers each. Sister received tens of thousands of these notes; suddenly she was a great lady. Today she'd buy this; tomorrow she'd buy that. Fancy brooches, silk hair-binding threads by the bunch, pendant earrings, wristwatches — she had them all. She always wanted to pay for the carriage now when she went out with Jade. When Jade tried to pay she wouldn't allow it. Sometimes they argued over this when other people were around, and it was very awkward. It seemed to Jade that she was being deprived of one of her privileges.

She wasn't the least envious of Sister becoming engaged, however. She had seen Sister's fiancé. Not particularly good looking, he was very tall, and wore a long blue gown with a black outer vest — like a merchant, or one of the petty gentry. Besides, Jade was too young to have any interest in things like husbands and marriages.

And so, while Sister seemed to be growing more affluent by the day, Jade didn't concern herself with where the money was coming from.

Before Sister left her, Jade attached absolutely no importance to the meaning of "engaged".

In fact she still attached no importance to it even after Sister got married.

But she often felt lonely. She and Sister used to go everywhere together. Because the atmosphere at home was rather dreary, they had been as close to each other as twins. Now, with one of them gone, not only did Jade find life dull, even her grandfather pitied her.

And so she seldom lived at home after Sister married, but stayed mostly with her mother. At times my stepmother would invite her to stay at our place.

Jade was extremely clever. She could play the *taisho* lyre — a type of Japanese zither that was popular in China some years back. She also could play the flute and the fife, but most of the time she preferred the zither. When she was living with us, my uncle always joined our musicales every night after dinner. We had a flute, a fife, a Japanese zither, a small organ, a moon guitar, even a dulcimer. But we didn't have a single genuine European instrument.

When these sessions were at their height, Jade also began taking part. First she played a tune, then joined in with the rest of us. Everyone thought it was good to have some variety in the old tunes we knew so well, after playing them every day. We pitched in with redoubled energy. The flute player made his reed vibrate so loud it nearly split. My ten-year-old brother played a harmonica, sweeping his lips across it avidly, as though he wanted to swallow it. No one was too fussy over what exactly he was playing. Suddenly courageous, everyone seemed to feel that noise was all that was needed.

Since we were playing faster and faster, the boy at the organ couldn't find the right keys. He just kept pumping the foot pedals more and more rapidly, making them groan. It was as if he were trying to wreck the organ, to rip it apart.

Probably we were doing *Plum Blossoms*. I don't know how many times we repeated it, but nobody seemed willing to stop. Finally we just didn't have the strength to go on. Some got out of rhythm, others lost the tune. At last we all burst out laughing and quit.

But somehow underlying this merriment was a tragic note. Perhaps great joy leads to sadness. As we laughed there were tears in our eyes.

At that moment we looked out the window. My youngest brother, who had just learned to walk, was coming to join us with a huge broken accordion on his back.

We knew no one could get a sound out of it. Everyone howled with mirth, and we became cheerful again.

My cousin (my uncle's son — a fine pianist) was also our best flautist. Now he put down the instrument and said to Jade: "You play for a while!" Jade rose without a word and hurried to her room. My cousin stared for a long time at her curtained doorway.

3

When Jade stayed at our place, she shared my room. On moonlit nights, the moon shone in brightly. We would talk until cock-crow, though it always seemed that night had just begun.

When the roosters began to crow, only then would we say: "To sleep, quick. It will be light soon."

Once Jade rolled over and asked me:

"Is it bad for anyone to marry too early, or only for a girl?"

We had discussed a great many things before, but never this.

We had talked about what kind of clothes to buy, what sort of shoes to wear, how to match colors, what stitch to use when knitting wool sweaters. When a hat was bought we criticized its slightest flaws, even though because of their location they weren't important, or didn't matter at all — in any event they had to be criticized.

At times our talk ranged a bit further afield. We might discuss the engagement of some girl cousin, or the marriage of some relative's daughter. Or the rumor that a certain new husband and wife weren't getting along.

Foreign-style schools had already been in existence in our county seat for some time then. There were quite a number of primary schools, but no college. The perennial topic of conversation was foreign-style middle school for boys. Not only Jade, but all the grandmothers, aunts and elder sisters were very keen on analyzing the students attending this school. That was because they were completely foreignized. They wore Western trousers with cuffs an inch wide. They spoke to each other in foreign tongues, saying things like "good morning" and "da, da, da". Even more peculiar was that they weren't shy in the presence of girls. On this point everyone agreed that it was better in the old days. A student used to get red in the face when he met a girl.

My family could be considered the most liberal in town. My brother and one of my younger uncles both went to big cities like Peking and Harbin to study; their eyes were opened to many things.

When they came home they talked a lot about how boys and girls attended the same classes.

This sort of thing was extremely novel. At first we all thought it was much too radical. But later because my uncle, who had a certain amount of status in the family, often corresponded with his former girl classmates, and since my father had taken part in the 1911 Revolution led by Sun Yat-sen, our family became quite "advanced".

We were all very unconventional in our home. When we strolled through the park or went to look at the festive lanterns on the fifteenth of the first lunar month, the male and female members of the family all went together.

We had tennis courts at home, and we played from morning till night. When boys from relatives' families came over, we girls played with them.

But never mind about that. Let me get back to Jade.

Jade had heard many stories about marriage to boy students. Right in our own county there had been several unfortunate matches. Some of the boys never came home again after the marriage ceremony. Others let their wives live in one room while they themselves set up quarters in the family study.

Most people, when they talked of these things, took the side of the girls, saying that studying had ruined the boys. The girls were neither literate nor students — it made the boys angry just to look at them. They felt their wives were in every way their inferiors, and complained that the matches had been made without their consent. Though marriages had always been arranged by the parents ever since ancient times, today these youngsters were demanding freedom to choose their own brides. Yet look at all the mad things they were doing even before they got their freedom — taking a wife but never coming home, or letting the wife live in a separate room. The boys had been ruined by all that study.

Jade had heard such comments from many people. Probably she also felt indignant, for she asked me whether it really was very bad not to study. Naturally I said it was very bad indeed. What's more she saw that all the children in our family — girls as well as boys — studied in school, and that the children of our relatives were also studying.

She therefore greatly admired me, because I was going to school.

Not long after, Jade became engaged. It was shortly after the marriage of her younger sister.

I saw Jade's future husband in my grandfather's house. He was short and thin, and wore a blue cotton gown with a black outer vest. On his head was a hat with earflaps — the kind carters wear.

That day Jade was also there, but she didn't know that this was the boy she was engaged to. She just assumed he was some guest from the country. Her mother called me aside and told me privately that he was Jade's future husband.

Soon Jade too had a great deal of money. Her fiancé's family was even richer than the family of Sister's husband. The boy's mother was a widow, and he was an only son. Just seventeen, he was studying in a private school in the country.

Jade's mother often told her that it didn't matter if the boy was a little short. He was still young. In another two or three years he'd catch up with her in height. She urged Jade not to feel badly. As long as the boy's family had money, everything would be all right. A marriage gift of more than a hundred thousand was paid, and Jade's mother turned it over to her personally. In addition, the boy's family guaranteed not to finalize the marriage for another three years. Since the boy was so young, Jade was all the more willing to put the ceremony off as long as possible.

After her engagement, Jade became very rich. Whenever anything new appeared on the market, while she didn't necessarily rush to buy it immediately, it would be in her clothes chest before very long. That summer, silver-gray tunics were very popular. They looked lovely on Jade because she owned several and always put on a new one when she went out. After wearing a tunic a couple of times, she wouldn't want it because it no longer looked fresh, and would only wear it at home.

At that time earrings with long pendants were all the rage. Jade had two pairs — one of red jewels, one of green. Even my mother didn't have more than two pairs, and I had only one. But Jade was rolling in wealth.

High-heeled shoes were also just coming into fashion. Not many people wore them in our neighborhood. My step-mother got a pair first. The next was Jade. It wasn't the expense that kept other women from buying them. They just weren't used to anything so modern. It wasn't easy for them to accept new ideas.

The first day Jade put her high-heeled shoes on, she was quite unsteady. The second day she was fairly accustomed to them. By the third day, from then on, she ran around in them very smoothly. They made her walk more attractive than ever.

When we played tennis, except when the ball was coming straight at her face and she raised her racket to ward it off, Jade rarely hit a ball. When she took her stand on the white base line, she remained on the white base line; if she stood in the box, she remained in the box. She simply didn't move. Sometimes she stood with the racket in her hand and gazed at the scenery. Even after everyone had finished playing and was either eating or washing his face, Jade invariably remained standing alone by the low fence, staring off at Harbin in the distance.

Once I went calling with Jade on a family in my stepmother's clan which was celebrating a marriage. They were Eight Banner people — Manchus, that is. The Manchus have very elaborate ceremonies. All the young wives in the clan must be present, and they make themselves up very colorfully. We Han people don't seem to have any social affair quite so ornate. Or perhaps I was easily impressed because I was only a child at the time. But take the clothes the women wore. They were as handsome as the evening gowns Western women wear today. And all the women had on flowered jackets — very long, and not slashed at the sides, because they were Eight Banner women. Date-red was the predominant color of the jackets, but there were also some in coffee, rose or purple. They were embroidered with either lotus flowers, roses or a combination of pine, bamboo and plum blossom. In a word, they were beautifully intricate.

The women's faces were powdered and their lips were stained peach red.

As each guest arrived at the door, the women formed a reception line. They were all my aunts, and each came forward to greet me and Jade.

Jade knew them well, and she hailed them each by

name. To me, they all looked the same, like the dolls a child cuts out of colored paper. I couldn't see any difference between any of them. They all wore satin gowns. They all had very white faces and very red lips.

Jade attracted a lot of attention. She went in and sat down beside a large mirror.

The women clustered around her. Perhaps she had never looked so pretty before, for she was really stunning that day.

It seemed to me she had looked better on other occasions, but the women all said that she was as lovely as a newly opened winter plum blossom. Although Jade didn't ordinarily use any rouge, that day she did, and she wore a blue satin gown with gold flowers that had been made in preparation for her marriage.

Thus surrounded, Jade grew embarrassed and rose to escape. With bold steps, she hurried into the next room.

How could she know it was the bridal chamber? Our aunts all laughed and called after her:

"Don't be in such a hurry, Jade. You'll be a beautiful new bride next year. Now you can only look the place over."

As we were eating and drinking that day, many guests came from other rooms to peer at Jade. Holding her chopsticks, she appeared lost in thought. Calmly and pleasantly, she gazed back at them, as if she didn't know they were looking at her particularly. Other women at the tables stared at Jade enviously for some time. Then their expressions grew cold. It was as if there were something they wanted to say but couldn't. After exchanging glances, they smiled and resumed their eating.

4

One winter's day, right after the New Year, Jade came to my house.

My uncle's son — my cousin — happened to be at home then.

Very handsome, he had a straight nose, black eyes and a well-shaped mouth. His hair was nicely combed too. He was tall and walked with a free step. He probably was the best looking one in our whole clan.

The schools were on winter vacation, and my cousin had come home for a rest. He would be going back soon, when school reopened. He was studying in Harbin.

Naturally, we began our musical sessions again for him. Jade also took part.

The musicale was very jolly. Even my step-mother, who didn't know anything about music, also attended, sitting off to the side. What's more, the cooks and the maids all stopped work to watch. They seemed to be observing us rather than listening to our music. Our parlor was jammed. No doubt even distant neighbors could hear the sound of our instruments.

The next day a neighbor who dropped in asked: "Were you celebrating someone's birthday here last night?"

We explained that we were welcoming my cousin, who had just come home.

And so our home became interesting and we had lots of fun. Soon it was the fifteenth of the first lunar month — lantern festival time.

Ever since my father supported the new forces and the revolution, boys and girls were treated equally in our family. When there was play, we played together.

When there was something worth seeing, we went to see it together.

My uncle took us — eight or nine all told — for a romp on the streets in the moonlight. The road was very uneven and so slippery it was difficult to keep your feet. The boys raced ahead while we, walking more slowly, fell behind.

They turned and laughed at us mockingly, calling us little ladies and old mothers, saying we didn't know how to walk.

Jade and I dashed forward, but we both kept falling. Finally the boys had to support us. But we refused to show any weakness. So it was less a case of them supporting us than of all of us advancing in a single line.

We soon arrived in the city. Hung with colored lanterns, the streets were crowded with people. Lion dancers, boats, dragon lanterns, *yangge* dances were in such profusion it made your eyes blur. It was impossible to tell how many of them there were. And who had time to look carefully? Your eye would no sooner light on one thing than it would be gone and something else would turn up, only to disappear also in another instant. Actually, it probably really wasn't anything so special, but at the time we felt that nowhere in all the world could there be such variety.

Huge flaming torches, hung up outside the doors of the shops, looked as big as coconut trees. Each one was brighter than the next.

We entered a shop run by one of my father's friends. They were very cordial and offered us tea, cakes, tangerines and holiday delicacies. But who could eat? We were too excited every time we heard a drum outside. There were so many drums and trumpets. Even before one band passed out of earshot, another would come by.

Since our town wasn't very large, we met many people we knew. They had all come to see the lanterns. Among them were some local boys who were going to school in Harbin. My cousin knew them and so did I, for both of us were then studying in Harbin. They promptly joined us. First they went to look at the lanterns, then they came back and chatted with my uncle and my cousin. I understood those fellows all right. They were eager to talk with us because our family was important.

And so, on the way back we had two more boys with us.

Whether we liked them or not, at least they wore clothes in the big-city style. Both were dressed in Western suits and wore felt hats. Their topcoats were knee-length, which allowed them a free and easy walk, and were infinitely better looking than the queer long overcoats resembling big padded gowns that were worn in our town. Around the boys' necks were neatly figured silk or wool mufflers. The boys seemed more handsome and impressive the moment they put them on.

Jade thought both of the boys were very good looking.

My cousin also wore a Western suit, so of course he too looked very handsome. As we walked, Jade kept staring at him.

She was a girl who combed her hair very slowly — every hair had to be in place. When she made up, she might put her powder on and wash it off several times until satisfied with the result. The morning after the lantern festival, deep in thought, she combed her hair more slowly than ever. Usually she had to be called two or three times before going down to breakfast. But on that day she didn't make her appearance until after the fourth invitation.

In his youth my uncle had been a bold fellow who rode horses well and was an excellent shot. Now, although in his fifties, he was still quite charming. We children all loved him, and he loved us too from the time we were very small. Poetry and essays — it was he who taught them to us. My uncle grew very fond of Jade when she was living at our house. That morning, breakfast was already on the table. Although Jade had been called several times, she still hadn't appeared.

"She must be Black Jade," my uncle quipped.

Everyone laughed at his reference to the romantic young lady in the classical novel *A Dream of Red Mansions*.

Just then Jade entered and asked what we were laughing about. No one was willing to say. Realizing we must be laughing at her, she demanded:

"Tell me at once. I won't eat all day if you don't. You're picking on me because you all can read books and I can't. . . ."

She raised quite a row. In the end, my cousin told her. My uncle was rather embarrassed that he had said such a thing in the presence of his son. But he drank a lot of wine and the incident passed.

Jade began wanting to study from that day. But she was already twenty. Where could she go? She was much too old for primary school. Middle school? She couldn't read a single word. So she just continued to live with us.

We played all day — musical instruments, cards. And

everyone took part — my uncle, my cousin, my stepmother.

Jade didn't show any special interest in my cousin. And he behaved the same toward Jade as he did to the rest of us.

But when he told stories, Jade listened more carefully than we did. Because she was a bit older than we, her power of comprehension was somewhat closer to his. He was a trifle more polite to her than he was to us. When he spoke to her, it was all, "Yes, certainly." But to us, he only said, "Right, right." Naturally that was because Jade was a guest, and she was part of an older generation than his in the family.

One evening after supper the two of them disappeared. Usually we had a musical session after the evening meal. No one organized us that day, perhaps because my uncle was not at home. After supper, we all just went our own ways. The parlor was deserted. I looked for my younger brother to play chess with me, but I couldn't find him. So I played the organ alone in the parlor. After a while I got bored. The parlor was too quiet. As I closed the cover of the organ I heard voices, coming either from the rear room or from my room.

I thought Jade must be in our room. I hurried in, to ask her to start a card game.

But she wasn't alone. My cousin was with her.

When she saw me, Jade quickly rose to her feet and said:

"Let's go out and do something."

And my cousin added: "Let's play chess. How about a game of chess?"

They came out with me and we played chess. This

time my cousin lost, though he always used to beat me. I thought it strange, but I was very pleased.

Not long after, the winter vacation ended and I returned to school in Harbin. But my cousin didn't go back with me. He had been ill earlier in the year and spent some time in the hospital. Now my uncle advised him to ask for another two months' leave and remain at home.

I didn't know much about what was going on at home after that. Only what my cousin or step-mother told me. Jade continued to live at our place.

Later, my step-mother informed me of something that had happened before Jade became engaged. I had a young uncle in our clan, about the same age as my cousin. He stammered when he talked and had no personality. He and my cousin attended the same school. Although he had been to our house, I don't think Jade ever saw him. At the time, my grandmother proposed that he and Jade should marry. But the boy's grandmother had refused. She said that the daughter of a widow wasn't destined to have a fortunate life. A girl like that couldn't have had a good upbringing, to say nothing of the fact that her mother had remarried after Jade's father died — a thing no decent woman would do. She didn't want a girl from that kind of a family. Jade and that young uncle were of the same generation, my step-mother said, and his family was rich. If Jade had married him she would have had money and position; no one could have abused her.

Jade now knew about this. Whenever she looked at my cousin, she couldn't help thinking that he must have the same opinion of her. She herself had the feeling that she wasn't fated for a lucky destiny. Besides, she was already engaged, pledged to be somebody else's bride. What's more, she was the daughter of a widow who had remarried. She said this to herself many times a day. She could never forget it.

5

After Jade's engagement, three years passed in the flash of an eye. Word came from the groom's family that they wanted to arrange the marriage. Jade's mother came for her, so that they could start preparing her trousseau.

As soon as Jade heard this, she fell ill.

But a few days later her mother took her to Harbin to buy the things she needed.

The boy who acted as their guide in Harbin was one of my cousin's classmates. My cousin had introduced him. The boy students lived on Jinjia Hill. The scenery was beautiful. Most of the foreigners had their homes there. The dormitory where the boy students lived had steam heat and spring beds. When Jade arrived with a letter of introduction from my cousin, the boys received her like one of their girl classmates. Moreover, they had learned all the politeness of the local Russian residents. Girls had to be treated with deference, so Jade of course was respectfully entertained. They invited her out to dinner and took her to the cinema. On entering a carriage, she was helped in first. When getting out, someone always helped her down. She was waited on hand and foot. When she removed her coat, someone took it from her. She had only to indicate she wanted it and she was immediately helped to put it on.

Needless to say, buying her trousseau was not a pleasant task. But these few days with the students were the happiest of her life.

She felt that college students were fine people. They weren't wild, or rude to women. They certainly weren't like her brother-in-law, who frequently struck Sister.

As a result of this trip to Harbin for her trousseau, Jade was even less willing to get married. When she thought of that ugly little boy, she was terrified.

My step-mother again invited her to stay at our place after she returned, saying that Jade's house was too dark and cold and that Jade was too lonely by herself, while our home was warm and lively.

Later, Jade's mother discovered that she wasn't too keen on marriage. She didn't have the clothes made that she should have, nor had she bought the various odds and ends needed. Jade's mother felt she ought to supervise and urge the girl along. She summoned her home. She wanted to have Jade by her side so that she could more easily remind her of her obligations from time to time. Jade's mother was one of those who believed that if you didn't remind young people from time to time they'd do nothing but play. What's more, the marriage was scheduled to take place in only two or three months.

Much to her mother's surprise, Jade was firmly set against going home when her mother came for her. She courageously requested that she be allowed to study. She said she wanted to study, that she had no mind for marriage now.

At first, her mother wouldn't agree, but Jade said that unless they let her study she'd never marry. Her mother, knowing how Jade felt, thought of many frightening possibilities. . . .

Having no alternative, she gave in. She hired an old scholar and put a few desks in an empty room in her own family's courtyard. Several of the neighbors' daughters also joined the class.

Jade studied there during the day and returned home at night.

Before she had been studying very long, she developed a cough and was in low spirits all day. Her mother asked her what was wrong. Didn't she like what they had bought for the trousseau? Did she want to go to our house to amuse herself? Her mother asked all sorts of questions.

But Jade only shook her head and said nothing.

Some days later, my step-mother went to see Jade. She took my cousin along. Their first impression was that Jade was a lot paler. She wouldn't live long, my step-mother said flatly.

Everyone said that she was studying too hard. Her mother also said so. She said that all girls lose weight when they are preparing to get married; Jade would fatten up after she became a wife.

Jade herself nodded and smiled. She neither admitted nor denied anything. She continued with her studies, and she didn't visit us any more. My step-mother called for her several times, but she wouldn't come, saying she had no time.

She got thinner and thinner. My cousin saw her a couple of times in her mother's home. But it was only while everyone was eating, drinking and making polite conversation. He was supposed to be visiting Jade's mother. Young men in our town didn't call on young women. It wasn't proper. My cousin didn't look either happy or particularly downcast when he came back. He played cards and chess with us as usual.

Finally Jade could bear up no longer, and she took to her bed. When the mother of the prospective groom heard that she was ill, she wanted Jade to go through with the ceremony. After all the money they had spent, wouldn't it be a pity if Jade died? Hearing this, Jade got worse. When the boy's family learned she was worse, they asked that the marriage be performed immediately. We had a superstition that the marriage could shock an ill bride back to health. Jade only wanted to die quicker when she heard this. She did all she could to destroy her health. She felt the sooner she died the better.

My step-mother thought of Jade and sent my cousin to see her, giving him some money. He was to say that this was a gift from my step-mother; Jade should buy herself something nice to eat. My step-mother knew that young people are rather shy. Maybe Jade was longing to see him and he was too embarrassed to go. Anyhow, they hadn't seen each other in a long time. What with Jade being unwilling to get married, my step-mother had suspected for some time that there was something between them.

A boy couldn't call on a girl openly. There was no such custom in our town. But since my step-mother sent him with her gift, it was all right.

The day he went, all of Jade's immediate family were out. A little girl cousin received him. The young man was a stranger to her. She had never seen him before.

Without asking clearly who the guest was, the little cousin asked him to wait and hurried out to find her grandfather. Probably she assumed that a male visitor couldn't be calling on anybody else.

The guest only had time to announce his name before the little girl dashed away. She hadn't even heard him.

Where is Jade? My cousin wondered. In the inner room? Jade must have heard someone enter, for she called out:

"Please come in."

My cousin went in and sat down on the edge of her bed. "Feeling any better?" he asked. As he reached for her forehead to see whether she had a fever, Jade seized his hand and burst loudly into tears, crying as though her heart would break.

Caught unprepared, my cousin was very frightened. He didn't know what to say or do. Should he try to protect Jade's position, or try to protect his own? He heard someone approaching the door. It must be Jade's grandfather.

With a calm smile Jade said: "You've come just at the right time. Your aunt must have sent you. I'll never forget her kindness. She was very fond of me. Unfortunately I won't be able to go to see her... I can't reciprocate.... But I'll never forget the days I spent in her house. Maybe she didn't think she was being especially kind, but I think she was wonderful.... I'll never forget.... Lately, I don't know why, I keep thinking that the sooner I die the better. Every day I live seems so futile.... Maybe people think I'm wilful. I'm not, actually. I don't know why, but that boy's family has been very good to me too. If I married him I'm sure they'd treat me very well, but I don't want to.... I've always been bad, since childhood. I never do anything I don't like.... This temperament of mine has tortured me right up to this day.... But how can I have everything my own way?... It's ridiculous.... Thank your aunt for remembering me.... Please tell her I'm not as miserable as she thinks. I'm very happy...." Jade gave a bitter laugh. "My heart is quite peaceful. I've had everything I could wish for...."

My cousin was dazed. He didn't know what to say. At that moment Jade's grandfather came in. While feeling Jade's forehead, he expressed his thanks to my step-mother and said they were honored by my cousin's visit. He asked him to tell my step-mother not to worry, that Jade would soon recover, and then she would go through with the marriage.

My cousin withdrew. He never saw her again.

Afterwards, he often wept when Jade was mentioned. He couldn't understand why she had died. The rest of us were also puzzled.

Epilogue

When I came home for the spring holiday my step-mother said to me:

"If Jade were really set against the marriage it could have been called off. Why didn't they say anything to me?..."

Grass is already growing on Jade's grave, emerging in pale green patches on the grave mound, attracting the white mountain goats.

Spring fills the streets and lanes of the town.

The warm sun has returned once more.

On the street, people are selling baskets of dandelions and young garlic. Children pull down willow tendrils and twist them into whistles, which they blow everywhere. The sound is low or high according to the thickness of the whistles.

The streets and lanes resound with the children's whistling. It's as though spring has been called back through their cupped hands.

But this period is very short. In the flash of an eye the whistle-blowers are gone.

Next, poplar fluff begins to fly, and falling elm petals cover the ground.

In our part of the country, spring passes quickly. If you haven't been out for five days, you find the trees in bud. If you don't see the trees for another five days, you discover that they've put out leaves. In another five days, they're so green you wouldn't recognize them. It makes you wonder: Can these be the same trees I saw a few days before? And you answer yourself: Of course they are. That's how fast spring goes by. You can almost see it. From far away it comes racing toward you. And when it reaches you it whispers in your ear, "I'm here," and then runs swiftly on.

Spring — what a rush it's in. Every place seems to be urging it to come. If it delays its arrival a bit, the sunlight fades and the earth turns to stone. Trees especially can't endure any delay. Let spring dally even briefly on the way, and many lives are lost.

Why doesn't spring come a little earlier and spend a few days more in our town? Then it could leave gradually for another town, and spend a bit more time there also.

But that isn't possible. Spring has only a brief span.

Girls in twos and threes ride by in carriages on their way to buy material for spring clothes. Eagerly, they ply their scissors, cutting out patterns. They want to become as beautiful as the images they visualize of themselves in their minds. Day and night the girls are busy. Soon they will change into their spring garments. But in none of the carriages does anyone see Jade.

萧红小说选

熊猫丛书

*

中国文学出版社出版
(中国北京百万庄路24号)
中国国际图书贸易总公司发行
(中国国际书店)
华利国际合营印刷有限公司印刷
1982年(36开)第1版
1987年第2次印刷
ISBN 7-5071-0008-1／I·9
00350
10—E—1618P

UNIVERSITY LIBRARY